My Wooden Wings

by, Rachel Callaray

www.callaray.com

For my dear, Beloved Grandpa Kubala who inspires me more than he could ever know. May you soar through life as if flying upon wooden wings.

I love you!

Rachel Callaray

for Josie and Kenna

Snow

Have you ever walked in a newly fallen snow?

Not city snow, but country snow. Wilderness snow.
No tracks interrupting the pristine,
maiden blanket of white.
A new world created within a few hours.
A world of new beginnings.
Not packy snow. Not crusty or icy snow. But silvery,
millions-of-pieces snow. The kind where with each step,
you kick and are immersed within a dazzling assortment of
tiny, perfectly sculpted, crystalline snowflakes.
Not full-sun snow.
This snow's light is blinding and cruel.
Not full-shade snow.
Then the shimmering flakes disappear.
It is dead snow.
I mean half-sun snow, where sunlight is filtered by bare-
boned trees or patchwork clouds, and the rays penetrate the
earth in a kaleidoscope of intensities.
Then you can see the twinkling
of every refractive snowflake.
Billions of flakes,
each bending and reflecting the sun's light into
a sea of sparkling diamonds.
This is my favorite kind of snow.
Silent snow. Hope snow. Forget snow.

6

1. MY BOYS

"The pigs are waiting, Walter," I called to my youngest brother. I looked out the kitchen window. Joe Jr. walked past the windmill toward the pig shed. Walter scurried about in the living room, putting away his toys.

Glistening and warm, I kneaded sticky biscuit dough, stirring in flour until it was silky smooth. Outside, Joe Jr. paced back and forth, buckets in hand.

"Now, Walter," I shouted.

"I know," he said as he darted past the door, pulling on a boot and throwing on his barn jacket. "I couldn't leave the Captain in the dungeon. He needed a rescue."

"You'll need a rescue from Joe Jr. if you don't hurry up. The pigs are hungry."

My brothers fed the pigs every day at the same time. Four o'clock.

Time for my mother's insulin.

I bent before the ice-box which held my mother's medicine, double-checking Dr. Winston's prescribed dinner-time dose from the ledger. A crash on the porch stopped me.

"Walter!" I shouted. I marched to scold my brother's laziness. It wasn't Walter.

"Rosemary!" I said, surprised to see one of my best friends. Her black hair, icy-blue eyes, red lips and high-society clothes clashed beside my work dress.

In the driveway, a light tan sportster crammed with teen-age boys beeped its nasal horn. Rosemary talked quickly and quietly.

"Vivi, we're going to see a movie in Hartford. You've got to come. I can't handle all these good-looking boys by myself." Rosemary peeked over her shoulder, giggling and waving precociously at her admirers.

"Come on, Rosie," called a boy in the car. "The movie starts in 5 minutes!"

"You can handle them," I said. "But can they handle you?

Rosie giggled again. Walter and Joe Jr. carried their slop-topped buckets to the pigs. It was past four o'clock now. My mother needed her shot. She needed me.

My brother, Victor, came out from the house, pushing me aside, carrying long, carved pieces of wood.

"Watch it, Skivvy," he said.

I crossed my arms, annoyed. "You watch it," I said. "You should be milking."

He stopped abruptly when he saw Rosemary.

"Oh, are those your skis, Victor?" Rosemary coyly asked. "Are you practicing your jumps on Sunday?"

Victor stammered, "Uh, yeah, Rosie."

"I can't wait to watch you jump, Vickie. Erv said the tournament will be in February. Are you entering?"

Did she just say Vickie? I looked at my brother who had been nothing but an irritable grouch lately. His cheeks shone bright red. I made a mental note.

"Uh, yeah. First prize wins mustom-cade skis, uh, custom-made skis." Victor rubbed his neck, embarrassed. "I have to get to the, uh, uh, barn." He ran past us, skis in hand, tripping clumsily down the porch steps.

"He's getting cute, Vivian," Rosemary said as she watched him jog away.

I cringed. "Says who? Look, I have to go, Rosie. My mother needs her shot."

Rosemary grabbed my arm and looked around urgently. She dropped her voice to a whisper. "I have important news for you. You should come, Vivian!"

My skin prickled, but I knew I couldn't entertain with Rosemary and her admirers tonight. Or any night for that matter. The boys in the sportster jerked forward in my driveway, howling with laughter.

"Rosemary, you need something?"

Rosie and I whipped toward the equipment shed. My father stood there, arms crossed over his layer of flannel, snow in his beard.

"Hi Mr. Hostadt!" Rosemary gushed. "Can Vivian come to the movie?"

"Vivian has work to do."

"Okay," Rosie smiled.

My father re-entered the shed.

Rosemary sighed. "I had a feeling you couldn't come. I'll drop off the news."

She ran down the path, bouncing lightly, but stopped and turned to me. "It's about Jeb, Vivi!" she laughed and ran to the car. A boy pushed open his door. Rosemary sat on his lap, and the car took off, spitting dirty snow and leaving me behind.

Jeb. It was about Jeb! The boy I had known since I was five and now thought was the most-handsome boy alive. I hoped the news was about Jeb and me. Not Jeb and Rosie.

In the kitchen, I reached into the ice-box for the smooth, glass bottle of insulin. Carefully, I pushed the needle from my mother's syringe through the bottle's rubber top and gently pulled back the plunger. I watched as the clear liquid filled the syringe.

The house darkened under the early winter sunset, and I followed the hallway to a small bedroom just off the living room.

"Mother, it's time for your shot," I said.

My mother rolled to face me. Although her illness had greatly changed her appearance, her beauty still struck me as clean as a freshly fallen snow.

"Hi, lovie. Who was at the door?"

"It was Rosemary, Mother. She was only here for a minute."

My mother nodded. "How is dinner coming? Did you brown the ground beef? And get the bread started?" She was still making sure I was on top of things.

I was.

"Yes, Mother. I have to get the biscuits baking, but you need your medicine now."

"You're getting prettier every day, Vivi." She reached out and stroked my waist-length, brown waves. "Your hair looks just like mine when I was your age."

I loved and hated moments like those. I loved my mother's attention and her touch and our similarities. I wanted more of them, all the time, anywhere! But I hated her memorizing my face because she would only get the chance to see it a few times a day when I tended her bed sores or sponge-bathed her rashes or changed her sheets or injected her with medicine. I should have gotten used to seeing her like that. I didn't.

I lifted my mother's house coat and disinfected a small area with alcohol. I readied the syringe and pushed the huge needle through the skin of her abdomen.

I breathed a familiar sigh of relief when the needle was out. My mother didn't feel pain like that anymore. I did. I felt her pain more and more every single day. I covered her with blankets, her thin silhouette hardly discernible against the dim light from the window. I turned on the lamp next to my mother's bedside table.

"Look Viv, a cardinal." We looked at the windowsill.

"I should put out more sunflower seeds," I said.

The cardinal stood tall and cocked its thick, orange beak as he watched us. His feathers shone rich with crimson pigment, his crest crowning the only source of color against a dismal background of wintry white and gray.

"Thank you, honey. Now you run off and prepare your boys a hearty feast."

"Yes, Mother."

I scurried into the kitchen, but not to prepare the biscuits. It would be completely dark soon, and I had to get to my rock. My skin tingled. Jeb.

"You're biscuits are served, boys," I muttered as I dumped the dough into a greased pan. Who needed individual biscuits? A biscuit loaf was good enough. I shoved it into the oven and threw on my boots and wool coat. I ran outside.

I grabbed a handful of homegrown sunflower seeds and tossed them onto my mother's windowsill. Knowing the boys and my father were in the shed, milking barn and tending the pigs, I ran to the end of our driveway and turned onto our narrow road.

I marched over a hill and down into a small ravine. At the bottom of the hill was a one-lane bridge spanning a frozen creek. At the base of the bridge were three large rocks and one smaller one. If anyone passing by had taken the time to notice, they would have seen that these rocks were completely clean of snow. That's because they served a secret purpose.

I looked over my shoulder and down the road. I was alone. I picked up the smaller rock. My heart leapt with happiness when I saw Rosemary's note waiting for me.

Afraid of burning my biscuit loaf, I slid the note into my apron pocket for a later read, and ran up the hill to serve "my boys" their dinner.

2. CHORES

The boys ran in from the barn like hungry wolves attacking one tiny rabbit.

"That's my biscuit!" Walter reached for the biscuit loaf just as Victor took the plate from his grasp. Frowning, Walter turned to the next bowl.

"I don't think so," said Joe Jr., grabbing the spoon for the creamed corn.

"Just 'cause I'm the youngest doesn't mean you always get the food first!" Walter didn't fight back. He picked up his milk and took a long, slow drink. He'd help himself to the leftovers when the initial fury to get food was over.

"Nice biscuits, Skivvy," said Victor, disapprovingly. Nonetheless, he hoarded three pieces for himself and loaded them with the heavy, golden butter I had churned last fall.

"Tastes the same," I said. At the last second, I added, "Vickie."

Victor flashed me a look of hatred.

Until three years ago, Victor had been one of my closest friends. I looked at him out of the corner of my eye, stabbing his food as if trying to kill it. We used to have so much fun together. Fishing for crappies or hunting for puffballs, anything was fun to us. Victor's wavy, crinkled hair and brown eyes resembled mine as did the color of his skin and set of his jaw. It had been more than once people thought we were twins.

But now Victor had lost interest in child's play. He had lost interest in me. He was milking the cows with my older brothers, Joe Jr. and Abbott. And for the first time, he had played an independent role in completing the summer planting and fall harvesting. Out to the barn in the early morning hours and baking till dusk in the cornfields, Victor's world was a man's world where sisters didn't belong.

Aggravated, I snatched the last sweet potato from Walter's fingertips.

"Dad!" he yelled as we stared at one another. Abbott watched with interest.

"Yes, Walter?" said my father. I didn't back down. My eyes burned.

Walter looked away. "Nothing," he sulked. "Can I have the biscuits, er, the bread please?"

Abbott snorted. I had won, but I didn't feel better.

"Did you hear first prize for the ski tournament this year?" said Joe Jr., flicking a bread crumb at Victor.

"Yeah," said Victor. He kept eating, ignoring the conversation.

"Well?" said my father, surprisingly. "What is it?" My father grabbed a bowl of beans as I cut my sweet potato in half and gave the bigger half to Walter. Walter smiled at me, his dimples friendly and loving. I felt better.

Joe Jr. waited for Victor to chime in, but he didn't. "New skis," said my oldest brother. "Real ones. Brand name and everything. Custom-fit."

"You practicing, Victor?" said my father.

Victor swallowed his biscuit. "Yep. But I won't win. My skis are too small."

"They worked for you last year," said my father.

"But they're supposed to be as tall as my fingertips." He reached his hands above his head, reaching for the ceiling. "Mr. Skalstad would give us new ones at a good price."

"Your own skis are fine."

Victor grimaced. "They're too small."

"You're growing, Victor."

"I know that! And because of it, my skis are too small! Skiing on skis that are too small is dangerous."

"You'll adjust. If you want new skis, you'll have to win them at the tournament. We don't have that kind of money." My father set his glass of milk down with a loud thunk. It meant the conversation was over.

Victor inhaled his food, leaving the table almost immediately.

"When can I start ski jumping?" asked Walter.

The rest of us looked at him, startled he would even ask such a thing.

"Who was it who almost cut his finger off baling hay?" said Joe Jr.

"Ahem! Walter," said Abbott.

"And who was it who was picking rocks and stumbled on an underground bee hive?"

"Ahem, Walter."

Walter was a magnet for getting hurt.

My father cleared his throat. "Well, Walter, I don't know if ski jumping is for everyone. It's dangerous."

"I could do it," Walter muttered. He crossed his arms.

"Could not. You're too afraid to even ride Musket," said Joe Jr.

"Am not!"

"Are too," said Joe Jr.

"Am not!"

"Are too," said Joe Jr. and Abbott.

"That's enough, boys," said my father.

Walter helped me clear the table. I was grateful my father noticed the large stacks of dirty, dinnertime dishes and at least assigned the job to someone else besides me.

I turned on our radio as we worked. To the music, I imagined swing dancing and jitterbugging, skirts flaring and hair bouncing to brass instruments and quick-paced drums. Swing dancing was the latest craze and Rosemary, who had more social life than the 1920's flappers, had introduced me to the thrill of ballroom dancing with a partner.

I grabbed Walter's hands and spun him around.

"Hey!" he giggled, not resisting.

"You learn to dance, Walter, and you'll have girls lined up to be with you."

"Yuck! No thanks."

Walter and I danced the entire song, his dimples flashing with joy.

As I finished, my brothers relaxed and completed their homework. My father read by the light of the fireplace in his favorite chair, just inside the living room. They looked so peaceful, resting after a long day of school and afternoon chores.

I gathered towels and a bowl of hot water. The hardest part of my night was just beginning.

It was time to disinfect my mother.

My mother's electric light beckoned me. Twice a day, I cleansed my mother's bedsores, and nightly, I sponge-bathed her skin with iodine to prevent infection.

The sight of my mother instantly calmed me, and I mentally entered a different place; a world of women, mother and daughter, girlfriends, soft skin and long hair, babies and breasts, powdery smells and clean fingernails, and in this case, caretaker and patient.

"Hello, Mother," I said. I leaned over and kissed her.

"Hello, dear. How was dinner?"

I wanted to tell her how Victor was so mean. I craved for her to hold me in her arms. But she had enough on her mind.

"It was fine, Mother."

I placed my bowl on her bedside table and counted softly as I added 30 drops of iodine. The antiseptic swirled brown, then orange, then yellow as drops plummeted through the water like skipping-rocks sink to the bottom of Turtle Lake.

I closed my mother's door, drew her shades over the dark, dead snow, and pulled down her sheets. She'd untied her housecoat, and I took a deep breath as I witnessed ribs, bony shoulders and discolored legs.

I silently cursed God and his obscene choices.

"We'll start with your left side, Mother," I said. It was the same every night.

Soaking my cloth with sunshine water, I gently cleansed her skin, stroking her precious body as I went, honoring every square inch. I helped her turn toward her front and checked on the bedsores above her protruding tailbone and hips.

"Small, slightly weeping," I said as I bent over and examined them. I sniffed. "But no smelly drainage." I felt the surrounding skin with the back of my hand. "Not hot. Nice and dry. No signs of infection." I dabbed them with iodine.

"You sound like Dr. Winston," said my mother.

"I should. He trained me."

I did the same for her right side and turned her to her back.

After refilling my bowl with fresh water, I rinsed my mother from head to toe, removing the betadine that could be irritating if left on too long.

Finally, I sat next to my mother and held her slender hand. I studied it; long, piano-playing fingers, soft wrinkles at each knuckle, dips between bones and the swollen network of traversing veins. Her hand was meek and small and utterly soft from the restraints of her diabetes, yet knowledgeable of all the life skills I was stumbling to learn. They knew when to plant the peas and beans. They could knit a sweater. They had changed thousands of diapers. When I had been sick, they had held me until I'd felt well. Her hands were slim, but certain of the skills of survival.

"Now," she said, breaking my concentration, "tell me about your day."

Yes! Someone who cared to ask about my day. How I dearly loved my mother! Silently, I apologized to God and asked for His forgiveness in cursing Him.

"Well, I made potato pancakes for breakfast."

"Mmm, sounds good."

"Haydie is in love with one of the chickens." I laughed as our Golden Retriever curled up at the base of my mother's bed.

"They'd have interesting children."

"And Walter almost missed the ride to school."

"Again?"

I nodded. "We worked on long division at school. And I found a mouse nest behind the wood pile."

"They always know the best places to hide. Erwin have any good jokes today?

"What do you call a bee with a new hair cut?"

"I don't know."

"Bee-eautiful."

My mother smiled. "That boy has a never-ending sense of…humor."

My mother's eyes twinkled and danced with each story. Each fact. Each description. I embellished details to the best of my power, enabling my mother to see, smell and hear the daily happenings of normal life.

"Victor's practicing for the ski jumping tournament."

My mother shook her head. "Does he look better than last year?"

I shrugged my shoulders. "Don't know. They're practicing on Sunday."

"I hope he's learned how to stop. I don't like that nickname Erwin gave him last year."

"Crash?" I struggled not to laugh.

"And Jeb, any news about him today?"

My mother knew what to ask.

"No news yet," I smiled, my note burning a hole in my pocket. "But someday Mother, I will tell you that Jeb Rettlan and I are to be married. You wait and see."

"I can't wait, dear. I take that as a promise." My mother coughed, a little sputter at first, but then raking spasms.

"Yes, Mother. I promise," I said, sure she couldn't have heard me.

My skin pinched like bare feet on a sheet of ice. We both knew she wouldn't be around to receive news of my engagement, or to see me wed, or to see me graduate from high school, or…I'd be lucky if she were alive when I turned sixteen!

Damn it, God! Why her? It wasn't fair!

I found it difficult to breathe. How could I ever live without my mother? I gasped to life at a knock at the door. My father.

"I'll be back at ten with your shots," I said, clearing my throat and giving my mother a quick, but gentle hug.

"I'm counting on it," she said softly.

I left my parents together for their nightly reading. As I closed the door, I stopped to listen. I heard whispers. After some time, my father began reading a new book, "Their Eyes Were Watching God."

3. THE NOTE

I busied myself with cleaning until ten o'clock. I drew my mother's insulin and went to her room. My mother lay in my father's arms.

"Mother, it's 10:00. Time for your shots."

My father undraped his arm from my mother's skeleton. "Good-night, Dear. I love you." He kissed her cheek and left the room for his own bed. He didn't dare sleep with her anymore. He feared he'd crush her.

I lifted my mother's housecoat and cleansed a different area of skin. I held my breath, inserted the needle and pressed the plunger. I covered her and kissed her forehead. The wind blew ice and snow against my mother's north-facing window.

"Good-night, Mother," I whispered.

"Good-night, Vivian. I love you sweeter than maple syrup."

I cherished this nightly ritual. "I love you more golden than a harvest moon."

"Mmmmm," my mother sighed. "That's a lot of love."

I closed her bedroom door behind me.

I filled the furnace with a thick chunk of sweet smelling pine and tightened the damper. Dressed in my nightshirt and thermals, my face and hands washed, I lit my bed-side candle, crawled into bed and shivered under the cold covers.

I moved my legs back and forth, trying to create some heat when I remembered my note.

I cringed as my feet hit the stone floor. Darting into the kitchen, I fished the note from my apron pocket. I sprinted back to bed. My candle glowing, I finally opened my delivery.

Dear Vivian,

Jeb asked about you today! He asked if you'd be down by the lake on Sunday. I told him yes. You MUST go! I'll be there with Anita Mae, probably an hour after church.

Do you think Jeb will marry you or me? I used to think me, but now I think you. If it's you, I'll want to be in the wedding.

Erv told us the ski jumping tournament will be the second weekend in February. There are twenty skiers already signed up, eight in the 15-and-under category. Lots of boys! Is Victor practicing?

See you Sunday,

Rosie

I shivered, but this time not from the cold. Jeb had asked about me!

I couldn't fall asleep with my heart thumping in my ears. I carefully folded my note and placed it under my pillow.

Still awake at 2:00am, I filled the stoves with wood. A bitter, northerly wind whipped beneath the light of a half-moon, and the house creaked and moaned as the walls grew colder. The house slowly surrendered to the polar air. I scampered back into my blankets and lay my head upon the pillow protecting my note. I closed my eyes.

Four more hours until my mother needed her shots.

Four more hours before I would face the world another day.

4. A BUSY SATURDAY

I awoke and pulled out my father's gold pocket watch from beneath my pillow. 5:45am. Exactly.

"Well," I said to myself, "If I'm going to see the ski-jumping tomorrow, I'd best get to work."

I braved the cold and filled a pot with water from the outside well, slow to heat on the back portion of the stove for my mother's morning cleaning.

I drew my mother's morning dose of insulin. Before administering her shot, I scrambled two eggs and started them cooking. I poured a glass of milk and set it on a tray prepared with a plate, fork and slab of butter.

"Good morning, Mother," I whispered, entering her room. I administered her shot. She stirred, and I told her I would be back shortly.

Without wasting time, I hurried to the kitchen, scooped up my mother's eggs and buttered two pieces of toast. I returned with her food and served her breakfast.

"Eat quickly, Mother. Insulin on board."

Timing was everything with diabetes.

"Now Vivian," Dr. Winston had taught me, "To give your mother the best care, you must understand what is happening in the body. Insulin's job is to move the free sugar from your mother's blood into her cells for the cells to use as energy."

"Okay."

"If there is no insulin in her blood, the free sugar can't enter the cells. No energy. If you give her the insulin and don't give her the meal, her free sugar will all be transferred into her cells. She wouldn't have any sugar left in her blood. Either situation is dangerous. Do you understand?"

"Yes, Sir. I understand."

And I did. I understood the illness very well. I knew the importance of timing, snacks and meals, and the necessity of insulin in the management of her illness. I had to admit, I was fascinated by the human body and the problems it could have. But even more so, I wanted to know more about how we could fight the problems of the body. Like fighting diabetes with insulin.

I headed for the kitchen to prepare my boys their breakfast. I cracked two dozen eggs into a bowl and fiercely scrambled them with a half-cup of milk. I sliced a loaf of bread and prepared it for toasting. Returning from the cellar, I put three slabs of ham on a frying pan and placed it on the stove. When I heard my father hitching the horses outside the front door, I began the eggs cooking as well. Ten minutes later, the boys returned, and I served them breakfast.

Victor stamped in and didn't bother to remove his dirty boots. I scowled at the manure on my clean floor.

"Problem, Skivvy?" said Victor.

"What makes you think I have a problem?" I said too quickly to fake disinterest.

"Your scrunched-up, scowling face? Or maybe it's the way you're standing, like you're my mother." Pulling out his chair, Victor stomped his feet in front of it. "You sure you don't have a problem, Skivvy? I'm just not convinced."

"Nope," I replied. Joe Jr. snorted.

My father walked in, missing the entertainment. "It's a nice breakfast, Vivian."

"Thank you, Father."

After the dishes, I visited with Dr. Winston, our Saturday morning visitor.

"I'm concerned about your mother's skin, Vivian. It is a perfect place for infection. We must try and dry out her bedsores. Are you cleansing her every day?"

"Yes, Sir. Twice a day, Sir. With iodine."

"How often are you changing her sheets?"

"At least twice a week, sometimes three if the sores are weepy."

"Good. Good. Are you able to help her change her position more? The more we can get her off those sores, the better chance they'll have to heal."

"I'll try, but it hurts her to move."

I didn't think that would help, though. She'd had those sores off and on for almost a year. It probably was a miracle they hadn't become infected already. Or maybe, I really was doing a good job caring of her.

"The sugar in her urine suggests she needs more insulin. Let's raise her morning dose to 12 units."

"Yes, Sir." I wrote this in her journal so as to not forget.

"I think we'll leave the other doses the same for now. I'll stop by on Tuesday to check her levels again. Watch closely for signs of infection. Do you remember them?"

I counted on my fingers. "Redness, swelling, white drainage, hotness of the sore, streaking red lines, fever or irrationality."

"Very good, Vivian. You'll perhaps be a doctor someday. You're doing a good job taking care of your mother." Dr. Winston stared at me, his mind recognizing something he had probably seen in me before. He shifted his weight uncomfortably. "But you know, Vivian, you can't save her."

"Yes, Sir," I said. But he was wrong. He obviously didn't realize how closely I watched over her.

Dr. Winston left.

"I'll never get to the ski jumps at this pace."

The rest of my day went quickly as I completed chore after chore to the music from our radio. Clarinets and saxophones of the Big Bands kept me company as I made seven loaves of bread, one for each day of the week. At 3:00, I began the laundry.

I sterilized my mother's sheets, night-shirts and housecoat with bleach, then rinsed them with water so hot, my hands screamed and reddened like raw meat. I strung my ropes through the basement, living room and hallway and hung the sheets to dry. Soon, the house became warm and steamy, fogging the windows and pinkening my cheeks to a rosy glow.

With my mother's linens washed, I served my boys their dinner, then scrubbed my father's clothes. I worked my way down the line of boys until Walter's clothes were clean as well. I went through three large pots of steaming water and used every inch of rope for hanging. The house looked like a Sear's Department Store, clothes lining the walls and suspended freely in the air.

My father, done with his work, was the only person who offered to help.

"Need some help, Viv?" His face was smudged with something brown. His eyes seemed puffy, half closed.

"That's okay," I said. "I'm almost done now."

"Thanks for all your work, sweetie." He gave me a smelly hug.

"Good-night, Father."

"Good-night."

At ten o'clock, I administered my mother's last shot, stoked the fires and collapsed into my frozen bed. My red hands burned from so much exposure to the bleach. I ignored the rare tear on my cheek and managed a small smile.

I had completed my weekend chores and could go to the ski hill tomorrow. I imagined Jeb, so handsome in his woolen jacket and sporting cap. Maybe, tomorrow, my life would change forever.

I thanked God for my mother and her endless supply of love, beauty and womanly advice. I thanked God for my father, insulin and Dr. Winston.

I entered my dreams.

Here, I rocked on a tree swing during an exquisite, sunny day of June. I was eight, and Victor laughed as he pushed me higher and higher. My toes brushed the magnificent oak's leaves, and my happiness soared. Mother sang in the garden, and my spirit flew like a pair of sand hill cranes, their wings outstretched and graceful, barking their gobbly call, soaring on never-ending thermals.

5. TURTLE LAKE

I awoke at precisely 5:45 and quickly began my morning chores. Before long, it was nine o'clock.

"Walter, Joey, time to go," called my father. He walked past me, straightening his only tie. With his hair slicked back, he looked handsome. Powerful. The boys followed my father out the front door, their hair slicked back too. All greased up for St. Olaf's 9:30 mass, they disappeared in our Model A Ford.

Abbott, Victor and I stayed home to finish the morning work. While the boys milked the cows and butchered a rooster for our dinner, I cleaned the morning dishes and listened to our radio. I sterilized my mother. And at ten o'clock, I administered her mid-morning shot and gave her a snack.

"There's a sandwich for you in the ice box. Don't let Father forget to give you lunch," I smiled. "I'll be back by two."

"Honey," she said, "cheer for your brother for me. And I want to hear all about it when you get home."

"I will. I love you."

I could have waited for the boys to return, but I was anxious. I threw my snow pants over my flour-sack thermals, pulled on my boots, and grabbed my skates, hat and gloves. Not forgetting my mother's favorite guests, I threw sunflower seeds on her windowsill.

Freedom!

Only one of my siblings had escaped before me. Victor. He was probably already practicing his jumps and talking ski-talk with the other boys.

The walk from our farm to Turtle Lake was a horseshoe short of a mile. I enjoyed every lively, twinkling, snowy step. My lungs burned as I walked faster, pulling the frosty air deep into my chest.

As I crested a hill, I could see the ski jump in the distance, perched like a look-out tower surveying its troops. The tamarack poles and pine created an interwoven skeleton that reminded me of railroad ties and track turned on its side, supporting the ramp above.

My pulse quickened as I neared. Everyone in the area knew of this jump, and no one missed the annual tournament when skiers from miles and miles competed to jump the furthest.

Boys intermingled, talking ski talk. Men smoked cigars. I stopped at Mr. Maus's concession stand, the smells delicious.

"Erv's gonna win this year," said a boy next to me. I recognized him from school.

Erwin got Victor ski jumping. In fact, Victor's skis were Erv's old pair. Erv was a Norwegian-bred daredevil who jumped farther than any boy under the age of fifteen within a hundred miles.

"I'd think so. I'd win too if I had a dad like that," said another boy.

Erv's father, Harold Skalstad, a Norwegian immigrant, brought the Norski love for skiing with him. Under his direction, the ski jump was erected in 1930.

I looked up at the jump which seemed so far away, reaching for the clouds. A spider-web of wires extended from the jump at all levels and attached to the ground and trees, preventing the jump from blowing over in the wind.

The boys must have seen me, because they did the same thing.

"How tall is it?" asked the boy from school.

"Fifty feet, but then you've got the 125-foot runway to consider too," said the one I didn't know.

"Is Victor jumping, Vivian?"

I nodded, feeling my face burn. I wasn't used to talking to boys.

The Hartford Ski Club consisted of about 30 men and boys. Not just ordinary men and boys, but risk-takers, danger-seekers, fearful-nots and daredevils. These men and boys made my heart go a-flutter, along with all the other girls' hearts in the county. One jumper in particular sent my own insides airborne as his skis left the take off and sent him flying 70 feet before touching earthly ground again. Jeb Rettlan.

I closed my eyes as I thought of Jeb. I remembered Rosemary's note, and my heart leapt to my throat as I imagined Jeb asking Rosemary if I would be there.

"Please, God," I prayed, "please don't make me a fool today."

I followed the path to Turtle Lake and was relieved to see Rosemary and Anita Mae already skating. I waved from a distance, and they zipped across the ice to meet me.

"You made it!" Rosemary's flushed cheeks flashed of health and good cheer. Her wavy, black hair settled in cozily beneath a soft, gray hat. I swear her face was a picture-perfect.

"Hi, Rosie. Hi, Anita. Have you been here long?"

"Only ten minutes. Enough to be winded." Rosemary giggled, her breath foggy.

I scanned the sparse crowd. We were early. "Anyone else here yet?"

She giggled again. "No, Jeb isn't here. But Victor is! He's cute, Viv!"

"Ugh," I grunted. Hadn't she already told me that?

"My mom says to ask how your mother is doing," said Anita.

I swallowed hard and found my ready-made answer. "The same. Her spirits are high."

"That's good. Please tell her my mother says, 'Hello'."

"I will," I said.

The girls and I chatted as we entered the ice. At first, I needed my arms desperately for balance. Soon, however, I raced along, my hair blowing and the air stinging my cheeks with prickles of heat. We laughed and skated figure-eights. I grasped onto this childish play with all my being, allowing my inner child to enjoy her life.

Suddenly, Anita crashed to the ice as she grabbed my arm and pointed toward the esker. A member of the Hartford Ski Club was preparing to jump.

"They're jumping!" Rosemary and I chorused.

We fiercely skated for the shore. We yanked on our boots and threw our skates over our shoulders. This was not a tournament day, so there was no fee, but all the members of the ski club were practicing.

Running to a crowd of spectators, my throat burned from the cold. The sun reflected off the hill's wintry white, and I squinted my eyes as they adjusted to the snow's blinding power. The hill had an ominous feel. I hoped the boys were ready. It was too dangerous not to be. We wormed our way to the front for the first jump.

"It's Mr. Skalstad," Rosemary whispered, her voice raspy and low. If she had been twenty years older, or he, twenty years younger, she would have won Harold Skalstad's heart. "He's going to test the snow first. He's so brave."

Anita and I looked at each other and rolled our eyes. Rosemary's crush was going on three years strong.

Harold Skalstad checked and re-checked his skis, then took them off to descend one-third of the way down the jump. He smoothed a lump of snow that could have thrown the jumpers off balance.

With little new snowfall this winter, he and Erwin had hauled bushels of snow up the scaffold early this morning. They'd dumped it on the ski slope and smoothed it out. But it had been darker then. With more sunlight, the lump stood out like a sore thumb, glistening in the sunlight with a life of its own. Mr. Skalstad shaved it mercilessly, the snow surrendering. Satisfied the jump was safe, Mr. Skalstad re-climbed to the top. He strapped his newly made, paraffin-waxed, maple skis to his boots.

Almost instantly, the crowd silenced, and all eyes turned to watch this local legend make the first jump of the day.

Mr. Skalstad stood straight, his ski tips extending perilously over the ramp. He bent his knees a few times, pushing himself upward in a forward motion, mentally preparing himself for his first jump of the season. Without warning, and as quick as a heartbeat, he raced down the slope.

I instantly held my breath and squeezed my fists. Rosemary squealed.

He leaned forward, bending his knees, and spraying snow from the rattling jump. Just three feet before the end of the take off, Harold Skalstad thrust his legs upward. He catapulted into the air and whizzed by, his body seemingly light and streamlined, his legs straight, his arms beside him and his expression bold and as tough as leather. I watched the green Hartford Ski Club patch on the back of his jacket plummet down the hill. Just as quickly as he took off, he landed smoothly on the runway and stopped himself abruptly at the bottom.

The crowd erupted into cheers and Rosemary screamed with exuberance.

"Brilliant!" Her blue eyes sparkled.

I watched Erwin greet his father at the base of the runway and wondered what it was like to be the son of such a powerful and talented man. Victor followed in Mr. Skalstad's shadow and soon, the three greeted a fourth with handshakes. I froze.

It was Jeb.

6. GIRLS DON'T JUMP

"There's Jeb!" Rosemary squealed. "And Victor and Erwin are with him!"

She scooted through the crowd and placed herself innocently on the hill, assuring the three boys and Mr. Skalstad would cross our path while they were climbing.

I panicked.

This was the moment I was waiting for, yet all I wanted to do was hide behind Mr. Heppe's announcing booth.

"But we'll lose our spot for watching," I pleaded.

"Come on!" Rosemary called.

Anita and I jogged after her. With twenty feet between myself and Jeb, I thought my heart would gallop from my chest. This was a boy I'd known my whole life, but he seemed like a stranger now. So far he hadn't noticed me. He listened to Harold Skalstad, who was probably giving last minute advice. Maybe they wouldn't see me.

"Hi Victor! Hi Erv! Hi Jeb!" Rosemary ran, waving wildly, joining the boys. "Mr. Skalstad," she said, lowering her voice dramatically, "Breathtaking jump."

Rosie looked at him with the coyest of smiles. She glanced at each boy, sharing her admiration, showing them the possible reward of her attention for a splendid performance. Victor's face turned a dark shade of crimson.

Jeb looked my way. We made eye contact for a split second, but I had not even enough time to smile.

"Vivian!" Mr. and Mrs. Milton, from Hartford Badger Pharmacy, had spotted me. Wanting to ignore them, but incapable of disrespect, I turned.

"Hello, Mr. Milton. Hello, Mrs. Milton. Pleasant day for some ski jumping."

"Ah, yes. Those boys have more bravery than I, that's for sure," said Mr. Milton.

"Vivian, dear, I always hesitate to ask, but how is your mother doing?" Mrs. Milton never hesitated to ask about my mother.

I nodded. "The same. Her spirits are high."

"Oh, thank the Lord and bless His holy name." Mrs. Milton thanked the Father and the Son and the Holy Ghost.

"Victor jumping today?"

"I think so, Mr. Milton. I saw that his skis were missing this morning."

"Good. That boy has potential. To take a Class C third last year after only two years of jumping was downright stupendous."

"Yes, it was." Why was everyone so interested in Victor?

"Oh look, there's Mrs. Goodright's girl." Mrs. Milton took a deep contemplating breath and shook her head disapprovingly. "I wonder if her sister had that young man's baby yet." Mrs. Milton straightened herself to board-like posture and aimed her nose for the moon. She gruffly grabbed her husband's coat. "Come along, dear."

I turned to re-join Rosemary just as Rosemary came to me. I peeked around her and saw the boys were now nearing the top of the hill. Jeb was gone.

"Ugh," I moaned. Instantly, the feeling in my legs returned. Relief!

Rosemary and I met Anita back at our spot by the jump. I quickly forgot my disappointment as dairy farmers, both fathers and sons, flew by to record distances all early afternoon.

Erv stood tall at the top of the jump.

"Dear God, please don't let Erv die today," said Anita Mae.

"Anita Mae! Don't say that word," I scolded.

Erwin's jump measured 59 and a half feet and elicited murmurs of approval throughout the crowd.

"You can see that boy is a Skalstad!"

"Wouldn't expect anything less from Harold's son."

I shivered as I imagined the pressure I would have felt if I were Harold Skalstad's boy. I had a new appreciation for Erwin.

"Look! Look!" Rosemary jumped up and down, squiggling and wriggling for a better look as Victor took his place at the top of the jump.

I watched with curiosity as Victor strapped his skis to his boots. "He told my father yesterday that his skis are too small."

Rosemary gasped. "They're not dangerous, are they?"

I shrugged. "My father said he'd learn to compensate. He said boys don't get new skis every year just because they're growing."

"Erv gets new skis every year," said Anita Mae.

"He's quite the exception, don't you think?" I said, annoyed.

I watched as Victor perched on his "too small" skis at the top of the fifty-foot jump. What if his skis were dangerous? Maybe he shouldn't be jumping.

"Anita Mae, do you mind?" I said.

"Dear God, please don't let Victor die today."

I felt a touch better.

Victor decided he was ready and took the plunge.

"There he goes!" Rosemary grabbed my hand.

Biting my lip, I held my breath as Victor ricocheted down the sculpted snow with unbearable speed. Nearing the end, he coasted off and flew into the air.

Unlike Erwin's streamlined form, my brother looked sloppy. With his knees slightly bent, he floated his arms out, trying to maintain his balance. He coasted by, and I could see his teeth through tightened lips. He was struggling.

Finally, he hit the snow with wobbly form, coasted to the bottom and slammed into a stack of "just-in-case" straw bales. He jumped up right away, waving to the crowd. He'd done it! It hadn't been pretty, but "Crash" had made his first jump of the season.

The crowd gave a mighty roar of support, chuckling and nodding their approval. I smiled, too, as I watched Victor meet Erwin and some of the other jumpers at the bottom. Victor beamed, obviously proud, and shook hands with those around him. I searched for my father. He wasn't there.

"Jeb!" Anita pushed my arm and pointed to the top. "It's Jeb!"

I turned to the jump and felt a touch of dizziness as Jeb latched his skis to his boots with leather bindings. I quickly prayed for his safety and thanked God for Victor's landing.

"He's going!" Rosemary shouted.

I opened my eyes to see Jeb plummet down the slope. Tall, straight, long and lean, Jeb coasted further and smoother than any of the other boys. At 17, he was in Class B, and sure enough, his strength proved his ability to jump with the older boys. He landed perfectly at 68 feet. The crowd roared!

Rosemary cheered with merriment. Once again, she grabbed my sleeve. "Come on! You want to be the first to congratulate him, don't you?"

Of course I did.

Didn't I?

My dizziness came back.

The two of us raced down the hill, and Anita Mae left to find her parents.

Jeb laughed with the boys. His skis off, he walked toward Mr. Maas's concession stand where sizzling hot dogs sold for a dime. Candy sparkled from shiny wrappers and one could purchase hand-warming hot chocolate for a nickel. Gentlemen purchased sweet-smelling cigars and crowds mingled amidst warm fires.

As usual, Rosemary let the boys know of our arrival. "Hello! Erv, your jump was fantastic. And Victor, your form was perfect!" Hadn't she seen my brother jump? "Jeb, you looked great out there. Sixty-eight feet! Is that a record for you?"

Jeb shifted his weight under Rosemary's attention. Rosemary had that effect on boys. "No, not a record. Last year I hit 72."

"Are you boys getting some hot chocolate? I sure am thirsty." I couldn't believe Rosemary's brazen request for a drink. I just didn't have that kind of nerve.

"I'll get you one, Rosie." Erv was the first to offer.

Rosemary flashed Erv her most winning smile. "Well Erwin, you lovely, kind gentleman, I'd be much obliged." She took his arm and smiled at Victor as she left with her escort. She didn't understand. My family didn't have extra dimes floating around.

Suddenly, I was very aware of being left behind with Jeb.

"How about you, Vivian?" said Jeb.

I turned and melted into a puddle.

"Would you like a hot chocolate?"

"I'd love…"

"She has to go home," Victor interrupted me. "Isn't that right, Skivvy? It's almost two o'clock, and you're supposed to be home already."

If looks could have killed…

"That's okay," Jeb said. "Maybe next time."

My throat tightened. "That'd be nice," I managed to squeak.

I pulled my father's hefty, gold watch from my pocket and sure enough, it was 1:45. Time had passed so quickly! My mother needed her two o'clock shot in fifteen minutes, and I still had to walk home. Maybe I should run.

"I have to go," I said blankly.

"I'm glad you could make it today, Vivian," Jeb said.

I prayed to God Jeb would always call me Vivian.

"I wouldn't miss it." This was my last chance! "You, you had a super jump today. It's so exciting to watch! What a thrill. I'd l-like to try myself someday." I stuttered.

"I could show you how," Jeb suggested. "I mean, not down the big one, but on the practice jump…if you want."

I stared at him, too stunned to talk. Victor was stunned, too.

"Not in this club, she won't." He turned to me. "Girls don't jump, Skivvy. It's too dangerous, and besides, you have to go home and take care of Mother, remember?"

I knew my mother was waiting for me. She depended on me to take care of her. He was right. Taking a deep breath, I turned to go.

"Vivian, can I walk you home?" Jeb said.

"You mean now?"

"You can't, Rettlan." Victor was insistent upon getting rid of me and keeping Jeb with the boys. "You have another jump coming up."

Jeb looked at Victor. "That's alright, Vic. You take my turn. You could use a little practice on your landing."

Victor grimaced.

Jeb took the skates from my shoulders. "Come on, Vivian," he said. "I'll walk you home."

7. ELEVEN, IT IS

We walked in single-file silence, weaving through the animated crowd. No longer was there the disapproving eye of my brother or the over-exuberant flirtation of Rosemary.

It was just me and Jeb.

We entered the path toward home and there was just enough space for the two of us to walk side-by-side. I anxiously wrung my hands.

"Thank you, Jeb, for walking me home. You really didn't have to. I mean, I know how much you like to jump and all. And, I'm fine, really."

"That's okay, Vivian. I wanted to."

He'd called me Vivian again.

We slightly faced one another, and I noticed the defined angle of his jaw. His farm-worked muscles reached like wires down into his neck and disappeared mysteriously beneath his woolen coat. Why hadn't I fainted yet?

I couldn't help but smile, and he laughed. We had not said or admitted anything, but we both knew. There was something between us. Still, I pushed the pace, worrying about my mother and determined to not be late.

"So what do you think of Mr. Mayfield's class?" he asked.

From that point on, small talk was easy. We talked about high school, our classes and homework assignments. We laughed over memories of our childhood and shared our excitement about the upcoming Christmas holiday. I felt so peaceful and kicked the light snow, it flickering and floating in the air like cottonwood fluff.

"How is your mother, Vivian? I mean, is she going to be alright?"

I nearly choked on the snowball in my throat. It took an awkward moment before I found my ready-made answer.

"The same." Ahem. "Her spirits are high."

I looked in the other direction, toward the farm, straining my neck and squinting, as if trying to determine something of life-changing significance.

Out of the corner of my eye, I could see Jeb looking at me, and I knew he didn't buy it. If only he could see for himself. He'd know then. He wouldn't have to ask. But I didn't want him to see her. She was too fragile and weak. Too vulnerable.

Jeb changed the subject.

"So, are you serious about wanting to jump?"

I stopped short in my tracks.

"You'd really do that? Show me how?"

Girls didn't do the heavy farm work. They didn't play basketball. And they certainly didn't fly off a fifty-foot ski jump. Victor had said it. We all knew it. Yet, here was the boy of my dreams offering to show me how.

Jeb kicked the lightly-sifted snow, perhaps appreciating the opportunity to rethink his offer.

"Yeah, I'd show you how, on the small jump. If you want to." He shoved his hands into his jacket pockets and looked unconcerned. But I could see him catching small glances at me, waiting for my response.

We turned up the field drive to my house, and I realized the night of work before me. After this wonderful day, I didn't want to return to my real life of chores, brothers and imminent death. I wanted ski jumping, hot chocolate and Jeb carrying my skates for me. I didn't want my real life. I wanted this one.

"Yes," I said. "I want to learn to jump. But, I don't have skis."

"What about Victor's? He said they were too small for him, anyway."

"He would never let me use them. And, if he knew you were teaching me, he'd tell my father, and we'd both get an earful."

We reached my front porch, and once again, nervously skirted beside one another. It was 2:05, and I had to get inside. Quickly.

"Is there any way you could use his skis without him knowing?" Jeb said softly.

"How would we do that? He's obsessed with jumping and practically carries those things around like a baby's blanket. The only time he doesn't have them with him is when he's sleeping."

It wouldn't happen.

I wouldn't learn to jump.

I knew it.

Jeb smiled a brilliant, mischievous smile. "That solves it. Vivian, we jump at night."

I could hardly breathe. I stared at this boy who was going to teach me to rocket through the air on maple-formed skis by the light of the moon.

He was wonderful. Spine-tinglingly wonderful.

"I'll meet you by the road at eleven," I said quietly.

Jeb nodded, knowing I meant we started tonight.

"Eleven, it is."

He took my skates from his shoulders and placed them gingerly over my neck. His hands brushed my hair, and my knees went weak. He turned to leave.

"Jeb," I said.

He looked back.

"Thank you for walking me home."

"Wouldn't have missed it for the longest jump."

I thanked God for Jeb.

8. LATE FOR MOTHER

I ran into the house, threw my skates onto the table and darted to the icebox to draw my mother's insulin.

"I'm coming, Mother," I called.

I was 10 minutes late.

And I was never, ever, never late.

My guilt perspired into small streams that ran down my back and gathered at my waistline. I swallowed hard and hustled into her room, injection in hand.

Surprisingly, she sat up in her bed, her sheets tucked in around her stick-like legs. She leaned forward, peeking out the door as much as she could.

"Vivian dear, I was worried about you." She studied my face, trying to determine if I was hurt or angry, saddened or just plain late.

I was never, ever, never late.

"I'm sorry, Mother. I was down at the lake, and I lost track of time while watching the ski jumpers." I avoided eye contact.

My mother lifted her housecoat.

"Did you have your father's watch?" she said.

"Yes, Mother. I did. But it was so exciting that I forgot to check." I prepared her skin, held my breath, inserted the needle and pressed the plunger.

"Did Victor jump?" she said. "You know, Victor needs to jump. It helps him."

I finally had the courage to look at my mother's face. Her eyes were slightly closed, puffy and lined with a thin red streak that traveled along the inner edge of her eyelids. She looked old and sad. Had she been crying? I sat on her bed to keep myself from crumbling to pieces. She depended on me. And I was late.

She took my hand and gently stroked the tops of my fingers.

"He did, Mother," my voice cracked. "He went for 53 feet."

I wanted my mother to feel good for Victor. She didn't reply, only closed her eyes and tightened her lips. I obliged with more detail, so she could complete the picture.

"There were hundreds of people there, Mother, and the smells of hot dogs and hot chocolate were delicious. Everyone was in their snow pants and warm coats, and sporting their latest winter cap. Victor jumped after Erwin. At the top of the jump, Vic was so intense. He concentrated, then, zoom! He was off!"

My mother's fingers closed just a little tighter.

"He went so fast, Mother! Down the slide, with snow spraying everywhere, and the sound of his skis racketing to the take off. Everyone gathered alongside the runway, holding their breath. I was terrified for Victor, Mother! It was so exciting!"

I laughed when I saw my mother's lips turn upward into a grin.

"When he got to the bottom of the slide, he threw himself forward and went sailing into the air. He looked pretty good, too. He floated right by us as if he had wings. Wooden wings." I would save him the honest critique.

"Please don't tell me he crashed at the bottom again," she said, one eye slightly opening.

I giggled. "At the bottom, he landed and stopped right at the pile of straw. Everyone shouted and cheered, Mother! Oh, how I wish you had been there."

My mother opened her blood-shot eyes and gave me her best smile. "I was, honey. I was there in spirit. And now, I even saw the whole thing. Thank you, Vivian."

I jumped forward, my heart breaking. I gave her my strongest, yet gentlest hug.

"I love you, Mother."

"I love you, too."

I smelled the warm disinfectant fragrance of her skin. I felt a tear wet my cheek, and I wasn't sure if it was my mother's or my own.

I vowed, then and there, I would never be late for my mother's shots again. "Vivian, honey, you should probably get dinner started."

I nodded and released my hold. She smiled again, and I felt her warmth embrace me from a distance. She was still with me. Even when we let go. She was all around me.

I walked from her room to the cellar. Staring at slabs of beef jerky, I felt a strength growing inside me. A pounding, pulsing strength.

"I can save her," I said to no-one.

At that moment, I thought I just might be able to do it. Because I perfectly understood that she loved me tarter than the first springtime rhubarb pie, thicker than a July field of wheat and with more excitement than a 53-foot jump on maple skis from atop the esker behind our farm.

9. PIECE OF CAKE

I was thankful for my chores that evening as eleven o'clock approached with torturing slowness. I was in a fabulous mood, however, and turned our radio louder than usual. Skirting to the music, I couldn't help but express myself through my cooking.

"A little rosemary for you, little chicken," I said as I smothered the rooster with spices. After stuffing the bird, I loaded the oven with wood and put the rooster inside. I prepared a second course of stuffing in a pan. The rooster was big, but not big enough for all seven of us. I needed more.

"Walter needs something sweet," I said to an empty pan. I prepared bright carrot pudding, shredding the carrots into slivers of sunset hues. I added sugar, a rich pinch of nutmeg and more than a double helping of cinnamon. I crumbled the remainder of a bread loaf, mixed it with butter and eggs and sprinkled it on top.

"Potatoes for Father," I sang, peeling our home-grown, cellar-stored potatoes and boiling them. I mashed and mixed them with our freshest buttermilk.

At five o'clock, we were 30 minutes from dinner. I couldn't wait to see my brothers' faces when they smelled my feast.

"Wow, Vivian, you've really outdone yourself," I muttered as my father.

"The best cook in town," I pretended to be Victor. "By the way, Viv, sorry for being such an over-stuffed idiot."

"Your sister gives so much of herself to our family," I said as my father again. "Let's thank the Lord for her hard work."

I giggled.

I thought of Jeb, and gasped. He was coming tonight to teach me to jump!

"Girls don't jump," Victor had said.

I thought of my mother. Who would take care of her if I got hurt? Guilt and stress raced through my blood vessels.

But, I was going to jump. I needed to jump. That is, if Jeb showed up tonight like he said he would.

The boys entered the house in a calamity, throwing boots to the porch and tossing offensive barn clothes in the basement. One by one, they entered the dining room. They rumbled to one another. I was invisible as I stood by the table in my lacy-white apron usually used for holidays, smiling.

Victor entered, and I knew my smile would not be noticed. Unlike most days, he glowed this evening. The boys jumped on him with compliments and questions.

"Hey Crash, did it hurt?" said Walter.

"What was Erv's final jump?" said Joe Jr.

"Your landing was funny," said Walter.

"You think you can beat him?" said Abbott.

Victor's jumping was all that mattered.

"Great jump, Victor," I said as I looked to my older brother. I received a short glance. At least it was something.

My brothers talked all at once. Even when my father joined us, the clamorous discussion did not calm. Though his eyes looked tired, they crinkled at the corners as he grinned at his sons. He had missed Victor's jump, but had heard the word in the barn.

We quieted for my Father's prayer.

"Thank you, Father, for every day we have with my wife, our Mother. Thank you for providing Victor with guidance and safety today. And, thank you for our extra-fine meal."

He had noticed! I struggled a moment to contain a new set of tears.

I served my boys their dinner. Their rampant grunts and continued talking through open mouthfuls was my gratitude. Not what I had envisioned, but I guess good enough.

"Can I have the carrot pudding, please?" asked Walter. It was his third portion. His dimples glowed in my direction, along with a little nod.

There it was. A satisfied customer. I thanked God for Walter and gave him a nod of my own. I needed to tell Walter I loved him more. I knew his daily afternoon visits with my mother were very hard. He was only 11. That seemed so much younger than 15.

While Victor visited with my mother, my father read the Sunday Milwaukee Journal. My hands shook as I washed the dishes, knowing my time with Jeb was nearing. Walter entered the kitchen and rolled up his sleeves.

"That's okay, Walter." I gave my brother an unexpected hug. "Go join the boys. I'll wash tonight."

Walter's jaw dropped. "Really?"

"Yeah, really. I need some quiet time."

Walter left much quicker than he'd entered.

"Why aren't you in the kitchen," I heard my father say.

"Vivian said she wants to wash by herself."

After a moment of silence, my father returned to his newspaper. I giggled with anticipation. It was almost seven o'clock.

After putting away my dishes, I routinely gathered my supplies and went to my mother's room. Victor left in a rush, his hand wiping his nose. I smiled at him as he walked by, but he avoided my look. My mother took a long, slow breath, her lower lip trembling.

She was tired and looked terrible. Visiting with Victor was hard.

"Here's a small snack for you, Mother." I placed a bowl of fall applesauce before her with a piece of bread. She ate it slowly.

"Thank you, dear," she said.

She rested while I disinfected her skin. I disposed of my sunshine water and rinsed her clean. It was 8:30 when my father entered.

"She's asleep," I said softly.

He nodded. "That's okay."

I crouched beside her bed and whispered so only my mother's ears could hear. "I love you richer than carrot pudding with nutmeg and cinnamon."

My father lay beside her and draped his arm gently over her shoulder. As I left, I heard him begin, "A Midsummer Night's Dream," my mother's favorite.

At 10 o'clock, I awoke my father, and he disappeared for the night. I gave my mother her shot and noted the dose in her journal. I kissed her warm forehead, turned off her light and closed the door behind me.

My night was just beginning.

The next hour was nerve-wracking. I found myself faint with worry. I knocked over a glass bottle as Victor walked by to go upstairs to bed.

"What's your problem?" he demanded.

"Nothing. Sorry," I said. He looked at me funny.

By 10:45, the house was completely quiet. I added wood to the fires and tip-toed upstairs to Victor's room.

"Please let Grumpy be asleep," I muttered to myself. "Please, please, please."

His skis gently leaned against a corner in the hall.

Perfect!

I gathered them, pressing them tightly against my chest. Listening for Victor, I started breathing again when everything stayed silent. I slid down the stairs, avoiding the creaky ones.

I put on my wet outerwear and snuck out the front door, peeking behind me, sure someone was watching. But no one was.

Hurrying to the road, I jumped as Haydie ran out at me from the barn.

"Haydie, go! Go on!" I whispered harshly.

Haydie jumped and played, daring me to chase her. As long as she stayed quiet, I would ignore her. I pushed past.

At the end of the driveway, I nervously approached a dark figure in the shadows.

"Jeb?" I said quietly, afraid and nervous.

For a second, I thought it was my father. He had to know I was out here. Fear stabbed my chest.

"Yeah, it's me." He sounded nervous, too.

"Oh. Okay. I, uh, got Victor's skis." We both stood there, Haydie crazily running around our legs.

"Great," he said.

He didn't sound great. Dread. It was dread and regret I heard in his voice.

"Look," I said. "We don't have to do this. It is…kinda crazy."

Through the filtered light of a halfish moon he said, "No, let's go."

Haydie ran ahead, then back, chasing phantoms of snow. We walked in silence, too uneasy to speak. We were almost to the practice jump before he noticed I was maneuvering Victor's skis from shoulder to shoulder. They were solid maple and heavy.

"Let me carry those for you, Vivian."

I loved how he said my name.

"That's okay. They're not that heavy." That wasn't true, but I wanted to participate fully, like my brother would be expected to. I didn't want special treatment because I was a girl. I was proving myself. To whom, I wasn't quite sure.

We approached the fifteen-foot high practice jump, located a quarter mile from the big one, and put our skis on the snow. Haydie disappeared into the darkness.

"Have you ever skied before?" Jeb asked.

I laughed. "No. I don't know of any girls that have."

Jeb laughed, too. "No. Well, then let's just start with balance and stopping."

"Okay." Whatever he said, I would do. Anything, anywhere, anytime. On skis, skates or on my head.

I was delighted when he said the skis were the exact right size for my height. I was fascinated as he instructed me how to strap the skis to my boots. Listening intently to his every word, I didn't really hear what he said. His broad shoulders distracted me as he fastened the straps of my first ski. His shoulders were twice as big as mine. Strong. The angle of his jaw looked more defined in the soft moonlight.

"You finish by pulling here." Jeb looked up. "Could you see that okay?"

"What?" I panicked. "Yeah, pull right here." I reached down and pulled a strap.

"Actually, it was this one."

"Oh."

Darn it! Pay attention!

I put on my second ski, and Jeb helped me stand. I was ready. He set me up at the top of the hill next to the base of the practice jump.

"I'll run beside you as you go," he said. "Just remember to bend your knees. Keep your skis straight. At the bottom, I'll slow you down and help you stop."

"No problem. Piece of cake."

Problem? Yes. Piece of cake? No.

I started down the slope and quickly picked up more speed than I could handle. Haydie nipped at my feet, and I leaned back too far, losing my balance. Jeb pushed me back up, however, at his own expense. He tripped over my skis and fell to his face.

"Snowplow!" he yelled as I skied away from him. What did that mean?!

I was on my own, careening down the slope with no idea how to stop. My skis seemed to answer for me as the tips angled outward in a V. I had no other choice. I crashed into a drift, bouncing off my right shoulder and sliding to a graceless stop.

Haydie jumped on top of me and attacked my face with her tongue. I immediately had an appreciation for Victor's accomplishment this morning, and I burst into a fit of laughter.

Beside myself, I shouted, "I did it!" Behind me, I heard Jeb's laughter join mine.

We moved to a smaller hill and spent the night practicing balance and snowplowing my skis to stop. At 12:45, and after many attempts, I finally made it down my drift without falling. I even came to a complete stop by myself.

Afloat with adrenaline, Jeb and I walked slowly to my house. I talked nonstop, hammering Jeb with questions about jumping.

We arrived at my driveway too quickly.

"I'll see you tomorrow at school," Jeb said quietly. We looked toward my house, hoping not to see a face in the window looking for me.

The house was dark.

"I hope we're not too tired," I giggled.

"I hope we don't get caught." Jeb looked at my house again. "You did a good job tonight, Vivian. We'll get you down that practice jump soon."

I beamed. "Sorry I knocked you over a few times."

"That's okay. A few bumps and bruises, but worth the ride."

I smiled. "I'd better go."

"See you tomorrow."

He walked into the night.

I ran, dying inside with fear of getting caught. Haydie sauntered inside the barn, finally tired. I peered out from the corner of our machine shed. It looked clear. Bolting to an oak tree, I hid behind the trunk, my heart pounding in my ears. Still no sign of my father. I tip-toed up the front steps and quietly opened the front door. I entered the warm darkness. No one. Farmers slept hard.

Quickly, but thoroughly, I cleaned Victor's skis. He wouldn't find out about my skiing by my own recklessness. I returned them to the upstairs hallway and stoked the fires. I lay in bed wide awake and could hardly contain my happiness.

I had done it! And it had been so easy. I tossed and turned, and a few times, laughed out loud.

I had actually skied. And Jeb Rettlan had taught me how.

10. HARTFORD HIGH SCHOOL

I awoke at 5:45 and crawled out of bed feeling smug. I wasn't surprised I didn't feel tired. I had been overworked and sleep deprived for over a year now. I had trained for this! The irony amazed me. I was a finely-tuned machine.

I laughed again at my unbelievable secret. What would everyone say if they knew? What would Victor think? And Rosemary? Or, my mother?

I finished my morning routine just in time to hear the horn of my father's Model A. I quickly checked on my mother and gave her a kiss good-bye.

"Ms. Lynn will be here at 10:00 for your shot," I said, knowing my mother already knew the schedule. "Your snack is in the ice box."

"Good-bye, dear," she said.

"I love you, Mother," I said.

"I love you, too."

Victor and I ran to the car for our morning ride to Hartford High School.

"Do you have the eggs?" I asked as Victor and I piled into the car with my father and Abbott.

"In the back," said Abbott. They would use them to bargain for groceries.

It was seven miles to town. I sat in the back seat, watching my father's head bob up and down as he drove over bumps and small snow drifts. It was a quiet time for me, and I had nothing to do but watch the passing fields and think.

I could think of nothing but skiing.

And Jeb.

Had it been a dream? I reached my hand to my right shoulder and massaged the soreness. My first fall. Nope, not a dream.

"When do you get report cards?" asked my father.

"Friday," I answered.

"Will I be seeing good marks?"

I looked at Victor. He acted as if he hadn't heard a word.

"Yes, Father," I said. "I'm expecting all A's except in History."

"You never get an A in History," said Abbott.

"Can't help it, I'm bored in History. History never changes," I said.

"If it's the same, then it should be the easiest," said Abbott.

"I like science and math."

"I got A's in history," said Abbott.

Had I had Victor's skis with me, I would've smacked him. Or the eggs. I would've thrown them at Abbott's great big, oversized mouth.

Rosemary always said I studied too much. The way I looked at it, I had to. While my classmates learned until 3 o'clock in the afternoon, I left at 1 o'clock, to get home for my mother's afternoon shot and to prepare for dinner. To stay in my sophomore class with my friends, I had to make up missed school-time and prevent my early departure from affecting my grades.

There were only a few more days until our four week Christmas Vacation. Most kids loved this time off from school. I dreaded it. School was my escape from seeing my mother so sick. It was a break from working every second. I lived for school. I couldn't imagine staying home all day.

Every day. I would surely die from grief and understimulation.

"Here we are," said my father, pulling up to Hartford High School.

"Don't forget," I instructed as the woman of the house, "I need to make Christmas cookies. And fruitcake. I need extra of everything. And if you want your sandbakkels, Father, I need cardamom."

"Cardamom. Yes. Anything for sandbakkels." My father grinned. They were his favorite Scandinavian cookies.

Victor and I walked into the yellow-brick school. But not together. The heavy wooden doors closed behind me. I breathed in staleness and people, papers and earth. Seven miles from my home, I felt peaceful here.

I couldn't concentrate on my classes. I found my heart racing as I replayed the previous night over and over. I kept my eyes open for Jeb, a junior, but didn't see him until we ran right into each other.

"Hi!" I said. He looked good. Brown sweater, tan pants. Freshly shaven. He smelled good, too. I prayed to God I looked even half as good.

"Hey, tired?"

"Not at all." I swallowed the huge lump in my throat. It was more intimidating talking to him in the daytime. Gosh, I hoped I looked good. "How about you?"

"No, I'm not tired." He smiled, and I nearly lost my books to the floor. "So, did Victor find out we used his skis?"

"Goodness, no. I washed and waxed them and put them exactly where he puts them. If anything, he'd only be able to tell because I took better care of them than he did." I giggled and shifted my books to my other arm. "I really had fun last night. Thanks again for breaking the rules to show me how to ski."

We looked precariously at passers-by. Nobody was listening.

"No problem. So, are you interested in trying again?"

"How about tonight?"

Jeb grimaced. "Not sure if I can. My pop's prize heifer is freshening, and I'll have to be there if she's pushing. Should I call you?"

This was a terrible idea! "No! We have a party line." It was too dangerous. Someone else might hear. "When will you know if you can make it?"

"By five. If she's not going by then, the night'll be fine."

I racked my brain for a way to communicate. Jeb lived over a mile away from me.

"You know," he said, "I drive by your place almost every night when I'm picking up my sister from her piano practice. About five-thirty. Could we talk then?"

It hit me!

"You know the bridge north of my driveway?"

"Yeah."

"There are three stones at the base of it on the south-east side. Leave a note for me under the smallest one. I'll check every night after dinner to see if you can make it. If there's no note, I'll just go to bed. Just like any other night."

"A secret rock? Have you done this before?"

I shrugged, a little embarrassed. "Well, yeah. Sure."

"With other boys?" he asked seriously.

"No! I-I, just with Rosie."

"Oh, you sure I'll know which rock?"

"You'll know. It's pretty obvious."

Jeb contemplated our plan. "Sounds good, Vivian." The bell rang. We were late for class.

"Three stones on the south-east side," he said. "I'll leave my note under the smallest one."

I couldn't help but grin from ear to ear. "I'll see you later," I said. "Maybe."

"Maybe."

We ran to class.

11. LIFE SHAPES UP

Jeb couldn't meet me for the next two nights. I anxiously checked my rock Monday and Tuesday, but there was no note. I also didn't see him at school.

Finally, during Wednesday's dinner, my father answered my concerns.

"Victor," said my father, "have you seen Jeb Rettlan at school the last two days?"

My heart skipped a beat. Could they tell my face was on fire?

"No, he's stayed home. I heard one of his cows was sick."

"Not just sick, but dead. Mr. Rettlan's prized heifer died during labor to triplets. He and Jeb had to cut her open to pull out the last one. All three made it."

"Cows or steers?" said Joseph.

"All cows. But with multiples, they may be sterile. Hard to decide whether or not to invest all the food and money into three cows when you don't know if they'll be good for milking."

Walter bit his lip, wrinkling his forehead with concern. He was always listening. "What would you do, Father?" he said.

My father set down his fork and looked out the kitchen window, contemplating. "I'd keep 'em. If they'd been from bad stock, maybe I'd think otherwise before I pumped a years worth of feed into 'em. But, if the three's fertile and can give milk like their mama did, that'd really be something." He nodded, rethinking his decision and reasoning once more. "Yeah, I'd keep 'em."

Walter smiled.

"Anyway, I hear those three calves have given the Rettlans a run for their money." My father laughed and snorted in a gruff, manly way.

So, that was why I hadn't heard from Jeb.

The phone rang, and I jumped with the rarity of it. For a brief second, I panicked, thinking it might be Jeb. We all quieted and listened as my father answered. He talked with his low, private voice, but we could hear some of the conversation.

"No, Betty, she can't travel. She can hardly even get out of bed. She's too weak."

"It's Aunt Betty," said Walter.

"Shhh," said Joe Jr.

"You think we're going to their house this year?"

"Quiet," ordered Joe Jr., giving Walter a menacing look. "I can't hear."

"Yes, Betty, Vivian gives her all her shots except the morning one when she's at school," said my father.

"Can I have the biscuits, please?" I said. I wasn't hungry anymore.

"Vivian will be here. School will be out. You won't have to give any shots."

My poor mother.

"Okay. I'll let them know. Yes, that's fine. Two nights are fine. I'm sure the kids would love to go to midnight mass…What? I don't know about that. St. Olaf's is a good church. It's our church. I know. Yes, I know. Well, it depends on the weather. We'll see you on Sunday."

"They're coming here," said Walter.

"You're just a regular Einstein, aren't you," said Abbott.

"Bye, Betty."

My father returned to the table. When he realized he had ten anticipating eyes staring at him, he laughed. "I suppose you want to know who that was."

"It was Aunt Betty," said Walter.

"Yes, they're coming Sunday afternoon, and they'll be here Monday night for Christmas Eve. They have to leave early on Tuesday to visit with Uncle Al's family. And," my father paused, the tone of his voice changing to something strained and uncomfortable, "they want to take you to midnight mass at Holy Hill."

My brothers and I looked at each other with wild eyes.

"Holy Hill?" said Joe Jr., sporting a scowl. "That's a Catholic Church."

"I'm aware of that," said my father, his voice rising.

"We're Lutheran," said Joe Jr., shaking his head.

"I'm aware of that, too," my father retorted.

"You're really going to let us go?" I asked.

Holy Hill was the most beautiful church in southeastern Wisconsin. Perched high on a hill and visible for miles and miles, it looked like a castle. Holy Hill was almost ten miles from our farm. Driving there in the dead of the icy night would be a thrill in itself.

"Well, I haven't decided yet," said my father.

Instant silence.

"We're not going," stated Joe Jr. smugly. He was probably right. I was sure my father would never go for the idea of midnight mass at Holy Hill.

"Is Gracie coming?" I said.

"Of course, Vivian. Grace is coming."

Another girl in the house! And Aunt Betty! I thanked God for my Aunt and cousin. My insides jumped with hope for a wonderful holiday and filled my very essence with cheer. Just having them here would make my mother happy. It was going to be a joyful Christmas. I just knew it.

My mind raced as I realized the workload of my next few days. Cleaning and cooking, baking and washing. By the time my relatives got here, I'd have it all done. I would.

After dinner, I did the dishes and packed a pot with leftovers.

"I'm taking these to Haydie," I called. But no one was listening.

I fed Haydie, then ran as fast as I could over the hill to the bridge. My rock stood out like an elephant in the cow pasture. I crossed my fingers and checked underneath.

A note!

I could just barely read in the dim light.

Vivian,
Sorry I couldn't come the last two nights. It's a long story. I can come tonight. I'll be there at 11. Don't forget your skis!
-Jeb

"Yes!" I squealed, quickly double-checking that I was alone. I was skiing tonight! I nearly leapt to the house. I hurried to gather my mother's supplies for her disinfection. My life was really shaping up.

I habitually went through my nightly motions, washing my mother and sterilizing her skin. I talked with her quietly and held her hand, relishing her warmth and softness. I administered her shot, and before I knew it, it was 10:50. I quietly gathered Victor's skis and crept out of the house. It was bitterly cold with a strong arctic wind. Again, I watched the kitchen window from the barn, expecting the light to click on. Expecting my father to be watching me. But he wasn't.

Jeb waited for me at the road. Haydie beat me to him, jumping on him, as happy to see him as I was.

"Hi!" I didn't try to hide my excitement.

"Hey, glad you could make it." He flashed me one of his smiles, and I had the energy of a thousand men at threshing time.

"I've been waiting to ski again all week," I said.

"Sorry about that. My dad's cow died in labor. She had triplets. We even had to harvest one of her calves."

"Sorry to hear about his cow. At least the triplets made it."

"It wasn't pretty. I can't believe they're all still alive. I've learned a lot about feeding babies with a bottle!" We laughed and walked to the hill. "We're worried they'll be sterile."

I nodded. "Is your dad going to keep them?"

"For a year. If it looks like they can't birth, then he'll get rid of them." I thought it was crazy Jeb's dad thought just like my dad. Farmers thought alike.

As we walked, I thought of my Aunt Betty's phone call.

"What are you doing for Christmas?" I asked.

"We're going to my Grandma and Grandpa's house in Oconomowoc. We always go there over Christmas Eve."

"Who stays home for the cows?"

"We'll leave Monday after the morning milking, and me and my dad will drive home Monday night and Tuesday morning, too. What about you?"

"My Aunt Betty, Uncle Al and cousin Grace are coming over."

"I remember Grace. She showed your cow with you at the fair one year."

I couldn't believe Jeb remembered that. "Yeah, that's Grace. I can't wait for her to come. I can't wait for my Aunt Betty to come, too." I pictured my Aunt's healthily plump body; a picture of the woman my mother should have been.

"My Aunt Betty is the greatest cook. You should taste her berry pies and fruitcake and log rolls. Oh my gosh, they're so good." Anything I didn't have to cook would taste divine. "Did you ask for anything for Christmas?"

"Not really. I think my parents want to give me farming supplies. They want me to eventually take over the farm, you know." Jeb quieted.

"That's great." Or was it? He wasn't acting like it was. "Don't you want to take over the farm?"

"Sure…no. Not really." He kicked the frozen surface. "I'd rather go to college. I want to be a lawyer."

"Really? I didn't know that about you."

"No one really does. How about you?"

"Oh, I asked for a watch from Knoll's. I always have to use my Dad's watch to keep track of my mother's shots. It's really big. There's this women's wristwatch at Knoll's, and well, that's what I asked for. It costs ten dollars, though, so I doubt my parents can get it for me. But, that's okay. I don't really need it."

"I mean, what do you want to do when you're done with high school?"

"Oh."

My face screamed with heat. Jeb was asking me what I wanted to do with my life. Not what I wanted for Christmas. My embarrassment suffocated me.

"I mean, do you want to farm?" He was serious. He wanted to know. He needed to know.

"Farming would be fine." I didn't think this was the answer he wanted to hear. And truthfully, it wasn't the answer coming from my heart. "But, I want to do something else, actually. Something no one knows about me either."

"What's that?" He stopped and faced me.

I didn't want to tell him. Sometimes my dreams were so big, I didn't even believe them myself.

"I, I…"

"Vivian, you can tell me. You can tell me anything."

"I want to be a doctor, in diabetes research. Like Dr. Fredrick Banting, who pioneered the discovery of insulin." I was Dr. Winston talking now. "His understanding of the human body, and his drive to help others, he's, phenomenal, a hero! He's saved thousands upon thousands of people. I want to do that too. Help others and make them well. Cure them."

"Like your mom?"

"Sure," I started walking again. I knew darn well I'd be too late for my mom. My eyes stung. I blurted, "We might go to Holy Hill on Christmas Eve for midnight mass."

Jeb looked at me funny. "Aren't you Lutheran?"

"Yeah. Surprised the heck out of me. But my Uncle Al is Catholic, and they want to go to Holy Hill. My father is considering it, but I think he'll say no in the end. Have you ever been there?"

"Not in the last few years," said Jeb. "We went during the summer when I was a kid a few times. We'd hike the trails, then picnic by the towers. You can see everything from those towers. And when you're climbing them, it seems…"

"…like you're going to fall right out? Yeah, scares the chicken feed out of me," I finished.

Jeb smiled. "I've never been to the midnight mass. Would your mom go?"

I didn't want to talk about my mother.

"No, probably not. Somebody has to stay home to stoke the furnace." Bad lie. Not believable. I sped up my pace. "Come on. Let's go!"

At the practice jump, I wasted no time donning my skis. Jeb wore his own skis next to me, perhaps having decided that his chances for staying upright would be better. The wind raked my face with its icy fingertips, but I ignored the burn and concentrated on the task at hand.

"It's darker tonight," I said, looking at the partially cloud-covered moon.

"Too dark to ski?" Jeb asked.

"No," I said, scanning the shadows. "It's dark, but not too dark to ski."

Bending my knees and steadying my arms, I moved forward until I started down the hill. I must have been a natural at skiing, because I made it all the way down before I came to a falling stop.

"Yahoo!" I relived the same feelings of exhilaration I had experienced on Sunday. I never wanted to stop skiing.

"Great job, Vivian!" Jeb stopped beside me and helped me to a stand. "If you can improve that much after one day, you'll be going down the practice jump in no time."

"And then the big one," I added. I gave Jeb a mischievous smile.

"I don't know about that."

"You just wait and see. Before I'm done, I'll be flying."

"Flying to the ground in a heap, if you're not careful."

I frowned. Climbing up the hill, I shouted back, "Not if I can help it! You just wait, Jeb Rettlan. I'll do it! I'm going to jump off the big one!"

"The big one's dangerous!" he shouted after me, his voice muffled in the wind.

The arctic weather didn't slow me down even for a moment. My time was so limited, I had to do what I could with every second I had.

Early Thursday morning, 2:18 to be exact, I lay in my bed, my cheeks fiery hot and my legs shaking from the excitement of skiing for nearly three hours. By the end of our evening, I was skiing down the hill and coming to an ungraceful stop, but mostly without falling.

I never realized before just how still the house was at night. My father didn't know. Victor didn't know. If anything, I should have probably been most worried that my mother would hear me.

The wind howled and shook the windows of our frozen farmhouse. Outside, all was deserted, a grayish glow illuminating the front yard beneath the light of the barn.

As I finally drifted into a deep, peaceful sleep, all of Hartford was unaware of the changes outside. The wind grew, engulfing the Earth in a ghostly roar. The cold dropped to a polar bitterness unsuitable for even the winter animals.

And beneath the light of the clouded moon, it snowed….and snowed…and snowed.

12. SNOWBOUND

I awoke Thursday morning at 5:45 with a crazy appeal for life. I couldn't concentrate for long on the memory of one conversation or run down the ski hill, rather jumped from thought to thought, my adrenaline still rushing from the night before. I couldn't wait to see Jeb at school.

Aware of the brutal winds battling the farm house walls, I grabbed a pail to fill with water from the well by the windmill. My best plan was to attack my increased holiday workload in stages.

"After breakfast, I'll start Mother's laundry, and make the dough for sandbakkels," I said to myself. "I'll finish them after school."

With only my boots and jacket over my housecoat, I carelessly opened the front door. I nearly fell as the polar air ripped the life from my lungs. Its bitterness stunned me to tears. Both the temperature and wind chill were below zero.

I gasped at the overwhelming sight before me. A world of white. A new world created within a few hours. A world of new beginnings.

At least six inches of snow had fallen already and a drift three feet high reached for my waist, challenging me to get my water. Violent snow whipped and swirled, gripping my long brown hair and wrapping it around my neck. Not able to see the well or barn amidst a pure whiteout, I outsmarted Mother Nature for only a brief moment and packed my pail with snow. I slammed the door before the drifts could overtake our cozy indoor nest.

"No school today!" I yelled gleefully.

I ran upstairs.

"Father!" I called into his room. "There's a blizzard! No school today."

He came downstairs quickly and layered up until only his nose poked out from his coverings. He opened the front door and bravely trudged out. I shivered and cringed as each of my brothers left, willing them to close the door quickly. It was one morning I did not mind that my chores left me housebound while my brothers and father went outside.

"Walter," I called as he opened the door, "bring extra firewood today. We'll need it." He nodded.

The icy wind had accomplished one thing, my scatter-brained mind had instantly turned to survival mode. My thoughts were clear. My father and brothers needed me. I fed my mother and administered her shot. I prepared my boys a hot breakfast.

Hash browns, scrambled eggs with ham, toast and hot coffee awaited the men when they re-entered the house having finished the morning milking.

Walter and Joe Jr. didn't appear quite as bad as my father, Victor and Abbott. Walter and Joe Jr. had worked primarily on feeding and milking the cows. Victor and Abbott worked outside clearing room for the cutter and preparing it to deliver the milk to the cheese factory. Their faces reddened in the steamy warmth of my kitchen, and the snow frozen to their eyebrows and eyelashes melted and dripped to the table. My father had spent his morning cutting more hay from the stack for the manger before the drifts were so high that one had to tunnel in for feed.

They ate ravenously.

"Are you sure it's safe to take the milk?" I asked quietly.

My father grunted, "The horses are prepared."

"The snow's only gonna get worse. Best to deliver now," said Joe Jr.

Ten minutes later, Gertie and Musket stomped in place as the milk cans clunked onto the sled and were covered with a half dozen horse blankets. My father and Joe Jr. disappeared into the white. I prayed for their safety and swift return, but knew they wouldn't be home any time soon. It would take far too long to get to the factory today, cutting new trails on the roads and plowing through drifts.

To calm my nerves, I started more water boiling for coffee, ready for the men to drink upon their return. I'd re-warm them from the inside-out. An hour later, I had to refill the pot as the water had evaporated.

Pouring myself a cup of coffee, I mixed dough for sugar cookies and ginger snaps while I listened to radio broadcasts about the "Pre-Christmas White-Out." I frequently called upon my mother to check my ingredients and make sure I was adding the right amount of this or a correct number of pinches of that. Actually, I just wanted to talk to her. I knew the recipes. At one point, I took the cinnamon into her room.

"Mother, would you please add the cinnamon? I never seem to get the right amount."

My mother gingerly took the glass bottle, tipping it ever-so-slightly, rusty-colored cinnamon filtering into the bowl.

"My favorite cookies, gingersnaps," said my mother, smiling softly.

"I know," I smiled back. I would have loved for her to accompany me in the kitchen, but of course, she couldn't.

I filled the oven with small wood chunks, steadying the temperature for sensitive cookie baking. I buttered my pans. The spicy smell of molasses cookies filled the house.

My father and Joe Jr. returned two hours after lunchtime, and everyone gathered at the table to eat my hot steak sandwiches and baked apple slices.

"Thanks for lunch, Vivi," said my father. He drank his coffee in big slurps.

"What took so long?" said Walter.

"We stopped at the Roleffsen's," said Joe Jr. "The horses needed water, and we needed to thaw out."

"Did she feed you?" I asked.

"Oatmeal, maple syrup and honey," said Joe Jr. with a smile.

"We tried to call, but the lines must have snapped," my father said. I ran and checked our phone. Sure enough, no tone.

The boys headed back outside while my father finished his coffee. He placed his cup on the counter and helped me gather the rest of the dishes.

"How is everything in the house today?" he asked, after peeking in on my mother who was napping.

"Quiet," I said, "but busy."

He patted my shoulders and went back outside.

I worked all afternoon. Walter restacked the wood piles twice as I went through them quickly. I washed my mother's laundry and hung it to dry in the basement.

Walter and I pulled out the box of Christmas decorations and hung them throughout the kitchen and living room.

"Remember this?" I said to him. It was a white doily with gold bells around the edges. It always sat in the middle of our Christmas dinner table.

"Mother made it," said Walter.

"Yep."

"Vivi?" said Walter.

"Yes, Wally?"

"Mom's not gonna get better, is she?"

I almost dropped the box. How could he say that? And at a time so close to the holidays. "Walter," I scolded, "you remember who was born this time of year and find your faith."

Walter turned away quickly, not speaking again.

We finished the decorations in silence and Walter went back outside. Clearing my anger, I got a head start on my weekly bread baking and stored four loaves in the cellar.

At dinner-time, I toyed with the idea of checking my rock, but knew it was useless. We were up to fifteen inches with drifts that reached the second floor on the north side of the house. My mother's window was black, insulated by a wall of solid snow. She worried about her birds.

"I hope they've fattened up from the sunflower seeds to make it through the storm," she said.

"I'm sure they did, Mother." Her black window was forbidding and grim. Dead snow. I thanked God I wasn't a bird or any other wild animal outside on a night like tonight. I surely wouldn't make it. I pulled down her blinds to cover the eeriness.

After dinner, I made a batch of fudge and sat in my mother's room with Walter. We cracked hickory nuts to sprinkle on top. My anger was gone, and my work was pleasant. The company of my mother reminded me of winters and Christmases past.

"Remember the year we made apple cringles and took them to the hospital?" my mother asked.

I nodded. "How many were there, ten?"

"I think a dozen. Some were still warm."

Those were the days when my mother helped others. The days when she felt useful, instead of useless. During those times we had worked together, ambling through the kitchen in haphazard patterns, creating sweet delicacies and tongue-tantalizing feasts.

Although my mother was now betrothed to her bed, her company brought me warmth and reassurance. Her feisty eyes sparkled as she told stories of her youth, my grandparents and their travel to North America from Sicily. Born Birgetta Re shortly after their arrival, my mother was never a foreigner.

It was soon time for my mother's nightly disinfection. I walked past my brothers with my bowl for sunshine water. They didn't get as much time with her as I did. As awful as it was to see her so sick, I was the one who spent the most time with her. I had never thought of it before as a lucky thing…being her caretaker. In a morbid way, though, it was.

As I cleansed my mother's skin, I suddenly found myself very tired. My eyelids turned to lead and fought to close. I sat at the kitchen table until ten o'clock, reading an assignment from school. I'm not sure how I did it, but I managed to stay awake and give my mother her shot at the right time.

Wearily, I stoked the fires and removed hot stones from my icy bed. I was so tired. Maybe, I wasn't quite as tough as I thought. Last night's skiing and today's busy day had left me exhausted. I let Jeb enter my mind and hoped the triplets were safe in their barn.

I imagined the ski jump as a frosty scoop of vanilla ice cream.

I couldn't wait to ski again.

13. CHUG CHUG CHUG CHUG

Even though the snow stopped falling late Thursday evening, the wind didn't cease until Friday night.

"How will Uncle Al and Aunt Betty get here?" said Walter at dinner.

Victor grunted. "Isn't it obvious? They won't."

"Will we still have Christmas?"

My father nodded. "Yes, Walter, we'll still have Christmas."

I got up from the table to clear. "It won't be the same," I said. The boys didn't understand how much I needed Gracie and Aunt Betty around.

Christmas was ruined.

After the milk was dangerously delivered Saturday morning, my father instructed the boys to feed and water the horses, but then re-hitch them to the cutter.

"What's he doing?" said Joe Jr., stomping out to the barn for hay.

Abbott shook his head. "Don't know."

Thirty minutes later, Joseph and Victor attacked the road with the horses and sleigh, pounding the drifts, trying to make some sort of track suitable for an automobile. Inevitably, it was useless. There was just too much snow.

We all sat in the house at lunchtime, deflated. It was quiet and no one spoke.

Chug Chug Chug Chug.

"Do you hear that?" I said, straightening in my chair. The boys listened too, their eyes growing wide.

Chug Chug Chug Chug

"It's Mr. Feutz!" someone yelled.

We raced faster than pigs scrambling for breakfast and threw on our outerwear. Walter staggered up the road to the top of our hill and came sprinting down through the snow, falling and stumbling through drifts and screaming the whole way.

"Mr. Feutz is coming! Mr. Feutz is coming!"

There was one machine that made that noise. Mr. Feutz's extended family owned the only large-sized John Deere in our neighborhood. In the summer, at threshing time, we could hear it from a mile away. We would wait for it to come chugging down our road, knowing ten or twenty neighbors would be arriving at the same time to help with the huge chore of thrashing the wheat and oats and barley from the stalks.

I ran to the end of the driveway with the rest of my family. Even my father was there, waiting for the huge John Deere to topple over the white-buried hill.

Chug Chug Chug Chug.

Suddenly, the powered tractor monstrously barged into view, spitting snow in all directions, pushing it off the road with a hand-made, wooden plow Mr. Feutz had constructed himself. He came down slowly, taking off his Santa hat, waving brilliantly as he passed our driveway. We jumped and waved crazily.

"Merry Christmas!" my father yelled and yelled. His eyes sparkled again, his smile lighting up his careworn face. It was the first time I could remember my father didn't look tired. He looked happy.

"Yeah!" Abbott screamed, grabbing me by the hands and spinning me in a circle. I felt my happiness soar as he let me go, and I flew into a pile of snow. Laughing, I watched my brothers throw snowballs and attack each other. They fought and pushed and wrestled like kids.

With the tractor now out of sight, we all gathered one more time at the end of our driveway.

The road was clear.

"Christmas is coming," said Walter, a splotch of snow on top of his head.

"Yes, it is," I smiled.

The rest of the day went quickly. I made four fruitcakes and rolled pecans with creamy nougat into nut rolls. Walter and I dripped hot maple syrup onto beds of snow.

"Walter, save some for Christmas," I said, pulling the pan away from him.

Walter chewed the candy, his lips glistening with syrup. "I can't help it. It's my favorite."

"It's like eating pure sugar," I said.

"Exactly," he chewed.

After dinner, I fed Haydie and snuck through the dark to the road to check my rock. This was not an easy task! As I neared the bottom of the hill, my heart leapt as I noticed the snow leading to my rock had been cleared. There, just visible, a small gray stone of lime stared into the wintry world, reflecting the moonlight, exposed and vulnerable to human eyes. How long had it taken Jeb to find it?!

"Yes!" I shouted as I found a small sheet of paper tucked underneath. The moonlight reflecting on the snow was so iridescent, I could read it right there.

Hi Vivian,
The triplets are alive and one of them thinks I'm her mother!

I like blizzards. No extra obligations. Just making sure things are okay at home. I can't meet you tonight. Too dangerous to ski. How about tomorrow? I'll pick you up at 11:00. If you can't ski, that's okay. I'll still come to see you.

~Jeb

I smiled and twirled, ignoring the cold penetrating the side of my boot. How would I ever make it to tomorrow night? I wondered again how long it took Jeb to dig his way to my rock. The thought of him tunneling through the snow made me laugh out loud.

I trudged back home to tend to my mother. Skiing in this snow would be difficult. A challenge.

"No problem," I said. "Piece of cake."

14. CHRISTMAS VISITORS

By Sunday afternoon, we were all very aware of the end of our driveway. Two o'clock passed. Three o'clock passed. Four o'clock passed.

"Maybe I'll try to call," said my father. But the lines weren't back up yet. "It's dead," he said, setting down the receiver.

Victor was particularly edgy, tapping his foot against the floor and opening and shutting his history textbook. He walked past my mother's room, peering in at the darkness. Her window was still covered with snow.

"This is ridiculous," he muttered as he passed me in the kitchen, stepping into his boots and yanking the door shut behind him.

"Yes, you are," I muttered back.

An hour later, I gave my mother her afternoon snack. Entering her room, I was shocked to be greeted by sunlight, breaking through her window for the first time in days.

"Isn't it beautiful?" said my mother, gently smiling.

"It is," I said.

I peered out and saw Victor shoveling his way in, scattering birds in all directions, anxious to get to the seeds on my mother's windowpane.

"Want some help?" I yelled through the thin pane of glass.

Victor shook his head.

"It's an early Christmas present," said my mother.

I nodded. Victor really did care. And he had perhaps given my mother her best gift of the season, her birds.

I was busy in the kitchen when finally, Walter shouted, "They're here!"

I quickly set my pan of quartered sweet potatoes in the oven with a large ham roast and ran out the front door to see Uncle Al shaking my father's hand and pulling him roughly into a big hug. Just the sight of Aunt Betty brought me to joyful tears.

"Vivian! Look at you!" Aunt Betty bellowed. She bounced up the path.

"Merry Christmas, Aunt Betty!" I wrapped my arms around her ample waist. It felt so good to hug someone and not feel bones.

"Merry Christmas, Dear." She looked me up and down. "Vivian, sweetheart, look at you." She pinched my waist, laughed and hugged me again. She went on to Walter who was waiting in line. I ran with snow in my shoes to the other side of the car.

"Vivi!"

"Gracie!"

We shouted and laughed, jumped and squealed, hugging each other the whole time. My cousin was my best girlfriend, even though I didn't see her more than three times a year. I trusted her with anything. Everything! I took Grace's hand and led her toward the house.

"I was afraid we wouldn't be able to come," she said, squeezing my hand. We giggled. Just in the joy of the season. With the happiness of it all.

Dinner started out extra special as my father and Uncle Al so gingerly carried my mother from her bed to a rocking chair which had been moved up next to the table.

She was there. My mother was at the dinner table with us.

Our whole family was together!

I felt as if my excitement and happiness would bubble out my ears. My mother smiled at me, and I knew it would be the best Christmas ever.

We all talked at once.

"The CCC has saved the lives of millions of families," Uncle Al preached of the programs of President Roosevelt.

"Yeah, but that's pretend work. Now farming, that's hard labor," Joe Jr. and Abbott bantered, pushing Uncle Al's buttons.

Uncle Al's face turned red. Joe Jr. and Abbott had to keep from laughing at his entertaining reactions.

"You'd be so honored to work in one of FDR's programs," snorted my Uncle.

"We're raising money to begin funding for a new female scholarship," said Aunt Betty, talking of the women's auxillary.

"What's a scholarship?" said Walter.

Aunt Betty ignored his question and kept talking. Walter nodded and nodded, listening to every word, shoving his mouth with food as Aunt Betty talked and talked.

Gracie and I giggled. Walter probably didn't have any idea what Aunt Betty was talking about. But he seemed to be enjoying the attention all the same.

Grace and I were caught up in a breath. I told her about watching the boys at the ski jump and the watch I so longed for from Knoll's. We declared insights and shared secrets. But, I wasn't sharing my biggest secret...not yet. I wanted to tell Grace about Jeb, but I just couldn't. It was still too dangerous someone would find out. And I wasn't risking anything.

Half-way through dinner, my mother moaned. I shot back to reality.

"Are you okay, Mother?" I said.

Had her eyes been so red before? Were they swollen now? She looked terrible!

"It's my legs, honey."

"Can I get you a pillow?" I said. "Or some tea?" I jumped up, knocking my chair to the floor. Everyone stopped talking instantly, focusing their attention on my mother.

"Joe," she said breathlessly, "Joe, I need to go back to bed. It's my legs. Ooooh." My father raced to her side with Uncle Al not far behind. "I'm sorry boys, it's just too hard. The chair is too hard."

"That's okay, Getta. Just wrap your arms around us, and we'll take you back to bed." My father, as hard and callused as he was from farm work, was as soft and gentle as a baby now. He scooped up my mother, supporting her head on his shoulder. She couldn't have weighed more than 80 pounds.

We all tried to act as if nothing was wrong, but dinner was over. My happiness had been clouded by the staunch fog of death. I put down my fork. I stood and cleared the dishes.

"Viv, honey, sit down and let me do that for you," said Aunt Betty.

"That's okay, I'm used to it."

Victor also left the room. My father returned to the table, and Aunt Betty went to my mother's room and closed the door. I was glad my mother had Aunt Betty during this holiday. I knew that for the next few days, someone would

be with Mother every second. She may not be able to
move. She may have to stay in bed, but she would not be
alone. Not during Christmas.

Aunt Betty came out a few minutes later. It was clear
she had been crying. She smiled too big and talked too
loudly.

"Whew, it's hot," she said as she wiped her brow and
eyes. I was used to my mother's appearance. I understood
how someone who hadn't seen her in months would grieve.

Between dinner and my mother's evening cleansing,
Grace, Aunt Betty and I sat in my mother's room and
talked.

"I just saw a Donna Gordon at Heppe's. The neckline-is-
gorgeous," my Aunt Betty exclaimed as she knitted a
stocking cap. "Ruffles everywhere and a flared skirt. And,
short, too! You'd think a skirt at the knee would be too cold
in the dead of winter. What women will do these days to
get attention. You'd think they all thought they were movie
stars." She shook her head, rocking, resting her elbows on
her wide bosom. I couldn't imagine Aunt Betty in a short,
ruffled skirt.

I looked at Grace, and we giggled. The thought of movie
stars in the dairy town of Hartford, Wisconsin, buying their
clothing at Heppe's Department Store was a riot.

"Speaking of movies," Aunt Betty went on, "isn't that
Charles Boyer a dreamboat?"

"Betty!" My mother looked at us girls, and we laughed.
Even Mother laughed! Big, round Aunt Betty thought
movie star Charles Boyer was a dreamboat. I laughed so
hard, I cried. My father peeked his head through the door.

"Hello, ladies. Is everything okay in here? I heard laughter, and that's a sound I don't hear all that often, so I just wanted to make sure."

Aunt Betty winked at me. She changed her voice so it was raspy. "Oh yes, Joe, we're all fine. Thank-you for checking on us. You're just a dreamy little dreamboat, aren't you?" My father looked puzzled.

The laughter was almost too much! Gracie leaned on my shoulders, and I hugged her close to keep her from falling to the floor. I looked at my mother and her smile almost disguised the bags under her eyes.

"Yes," my mother said, "quite dreamy." My father sprinted in and kissed her on the forehead.

"Keep yourselves in check here, ladies," he ordered with a military tone.

"Yes, Sir!" I yelled.

"Dreamboat!" shouted Grace.

Sweet laughter.

Soon enough, the party broke, and I gave my mother her nightly cleansing. She sang Christmas carols and seemed to be in less pain. Perhaps it was from the laughter.

We loaded the fireplace in the living room and set up a makeshift mattress of couch pillows and blankets on the floor for Grace. My father would sleep on the floor in my mother's room, and Uncle Al and Aunt Betty took their bags upstairs. It was a full house. Even more full than normal.

Eleven o'clock came quickly, too. I didn't know what to do. Grace was still awake, reading by the fire in the living room. Skiing obviously wasn't going to happen. I knew I'd have to keep my visit with Jeb short. Grace would wait for me to return.

I bundled up. "I'm going outside to check on Haydie," I said. I wrapped my scarf and tucked it into my jacket.

"Now?" said Grace. "It's 11 o'clock."

"Yeah, sometimes she needs extra straw for bedding. I worry about her."

"Didn't you give her some at supper?" she said.

"She might need more."

"It's freezing outside, Vivi." Grace watched me. "But it's warm in the barn. Haydie will be fine."

"I know. I just like to check."

She was still and silent. Not Grace-like.

Without anything more, I slipped outside. I was about to walk past the barn when I peeked back at the house. Grace's face appeared in the kitchen window. I ducked into the barn and tripped over Haydie, who playfully rammed my legs. I fumbled my way out through the west-side door and ran to the road. Jeb was waiting.

"Hi!" My heart beat like a thousand hummingbird wings.

"Hi, Vivian." Jeb had his skis. "No skiing tonight?"

"No, I'm sorry. I can't. Gracie's here, and I'm too afraid someone will find out. She's waiting for me right now. I said I was checking on Haydie."

"That's okay, Vivian. How is Grace?"

"She's just as sweet as ever. I love having another girl in the house. And my Aunt Betty, she made us laugh all night. She even called my father a dreamboat." I giggled.

"You're pretty, Vivian," said Jeb.

I caught my breath and felt a prickly burn creep up my neck to my face.

"I mean it. I think you're a pretty girl."

I didn't know what to say. "Thanks."

"You're welcome. Well," he looked up the hill into the darkness, "I should probably get going before Grace gets suspicious. Tomorrow is Christmas Eve. Are you still planning on going to Holy Hill for midnight mass?"

"Not sure. It depends on my father. If not, we'll be at St. Olaf's."

"Okay, well, Merry Christmas, Vivian." Suddenly Jeb leaned forward and kissed me on the cheek. Just a small kiss, but a kiss, nonetheless.

My voice quivered. "Merry Christmas, Jeb. Will I see you Tuesday night?"

Jeb walked up the hill from my driveway. "Yes, Tuesday night. Eleven o'clock."

"I'll be here!" I called.

"Bring your skis next time."

"For the big one, right?" I said.

"I'm not sure about that. Merry Christmas!" Jeb disappeared.

I stood there for a while, watching the blackness and feeling the tingling warmth of my toes all the way up to the burning spot on my cheek where I had received my first kiss. I touched it with my hand and couldn't believe my wonderful night. Laughter, Grace, my mother, Aunt Betty, Jeb, a kiss, a kiss. A kiss.

I ran up the driveway and slipped into the house. I had completely forgotten about Grace, and I jumped when I she approached me from the kitchen. Her arms were crossed and her face, curious.

"What were you doing in the road, Viv?"

15. A SECRET IS OUT

I stared at Gracie, my cheek still burning from Jeb's kiss.

"I was checking Haydie," I said.

"In the road?" Grace shifted her weight. She looked cross. She knew I was lying.

I looked up the hallway, into the living room and listened for sounds of life. My mother and father were still asleep.

"Okay," I whispered. "I'll tell you. BUT, you have to swear on your family's bible that you won't tell anyone. I mean ANYONE! If you tell anyone my secret, my life will be over and I'll never be your friend or talk to you again. And I won't even go to your wedding."

Gracie's eyes grew large. She wasn't expecting something of such grand magnitude. "What is it, Vivi? What are you up to?"

I grabbed Gracie's arm and pulled her to the fireplace. The oak logs slowly sizzled and popped, and the bright orange coals glowed and warmed my skin.

"I have a secret." I whispered even softer now. We leaned in closely to each other, and I could feel Gracie's breath. The suspense nearly choked me, and I couldn't believe how my heart was racing. Pounding! I didn't know where to start.

"Vivian, please, tell me what's happening."

"Do you remember Jeb Rettlan?"

"Yes. He's older than us. When we showed your cow at the fair, he was there."

"Yes! That's him. Well, I'm seeing him...secretively."

"Vivian!" Gracie squealed. "At night? In the road?"

"There's a very good reason. He's teaching me to do something that girls aren't really supposed to do. We don't want anyone to find out. It's more than that, really, it's the only free time I have and the only time I can use Victor's…" I stopped. This was it.

Gracie shook her head and opened her eyes even further. "Victor's what, Vivian? His what?"

"His skis."

"His skis? What on Earth are you doing with Victor's skis?"

"I'm skiing. Even better! I'm learning how to jump! You know, off the ski jump behind the farm."

"The big one? Vivian, isn't that dangerous?"

"Well, I'm not going down the big one, yet. We're just starting with hills and stopping. Next time, I'm trying the practice jump. Jeb doesn't know it yet, but I am."

Gracie stared, open-mouthed.

I giggled.

"And…" I led her on.

"And what? Oh, Vivian. Stop teasing me!"

"Tonight he kissed me!" I rolled back onto the floor and put my hand to my cheek. I snickered and rolled in the light of the fire.

"Where?" Gracie grabbed my arm, tumbling beside me. "On the lips? Vivian, he kissed you! Your first, real kiss!"

"He kissed me on the cheek. Not the lips. But, Jeb kissed me. And he said I was pretty."

We laughed and hugged, and I told her all about how I had been sneaking out of the house with Victor's skis. I told her how Victor had said, 'Girls don't jump,' and how Jeb had then offered to show me how. I told her how he had walked me home and carried my skates. I told her we were meeting on Tuesday night, eleven o'clock.

"But what if Victor finds out? Or your dad? You'll get in trouble."

I nodded. "I'm not planning on telling anyone, and Jeb isn't either. You're the only other person that knows. Can you keep my secret, Gracie?"

Gracie sat taller and put out her hand. I shook it.

"My lips are sealed, Viv. Your secret is safe with me."

16. CHRISTMAS EVE

Monday morning came, and we spent our time finally making sandbakkels. They were a persnickety cookie to make, and I was grateful to have helping hands.

"Walter," I said, "Will you please take these into Mother's room?" I handed him the tins. We moved everything into Mother's room. Even my father stopped by.

"How is the cookie factory?" he asked.

"Just fine, dear." My mother handed him a ball of the delicately seasoned dough.

"Not too thick, Joey," said Aunt Betty. "And not too thin, either. We don't want them to burn."

He gently pressed the dough to the inside of the tin until it was even throughout.

"Nice job," said my mother. My father kissed her cheek and headed out. We made five dozen of the ridged, cup-like, Scandinavian confections. It took all morning.

After lunch, Aunt Betty, Gracie and I began the task of making our Christmas Eve dinner. My aunt and father pulled a thawed ham from the cellar.

"Vivi, dear, hand me the maple syrup please," said Aunt Betty.

She poured a thick layer of syrup over the ham. Gracie and I sprinkled on cinnamon and cloves. We added sliced apples and sweet potatoes all around and covered the pan before placing it into the oven.

We made corn bread and currant muffins. Mashed potatoes, rutabagas, mint jelly and green bean casserole. The food just kept coming.

"Plum pudding, Walter," I called into the living room. Walter sprinted into the kitchen, sticking his fingers into the bowl. "Not until you've washed them, Wally," I ordered.

Walter washed his hands, returning for his favorite part of Christmas cooking, tossing the plum pudding.

Walter squeezed and tossed raisins, currants, orange peel, carrot shavings and bread crumbs with flour, butter, sugar, cinnamon and eggs.

"How's that, Vivi?" Walter asked, showing me the bowl.

"Looks good," I said.

Walter licked his hands. "Tastes good, too." He leaned against my back, enjoying the taste of his spiced skin. He felt warm and small.

"It'll taste even better when it's cooked." I kissed his head.

"Are you done, Vivi? I think I need a break here. Get it? Knead a break?" asked Grace. She kneaded "Grandma Bread," a recipe for bread that had traveled with my mother's mother from Sicily.

"Yep, just have to get this steaming." I finished preparing the plum pudding and relieved Gracie's position of kneading the bread.

"Thanks," she said, massaging her buttery hands.

"You bet."

The ingredients of Grandma Bread were nothing special, but the process of making it was. It was kneaded and allowed to rise many times until the consistency of the dough was like silken fabric between your fingers. It shone and stretched and glistened with butter. We broke the dough into three balls and placed them into a pie-plate. It rested for fifteen minutes before we brushed it with egg and baked it in the oven for 40 minutes.

It was after the evening milking time when we all gathered around the kitchen table for our Christmas Eve finery. This time, the couch had been pulled up to the table, and my father and Uncle Al carried my mother out to join her family a second time. This time, the couch was soft. My mother could do it.

With my mother at the table, I was overwhelmed with emotion. Even for Victor. Here we all were, my family complete, my Gracie too, for Christmas Eve dinner. I wanted to stop time.

"Dear Lord," my father began, "we are here at a table dressed with the finest of foods. We have been blessed with the company of family. Thank you, for my precious wife, our mother and her continuing fight to stay with us. Thank you for Dr. Frederick Banting, Mr. Best, Dr. Collip and Professor Macleod and their brilliant discovery of insulin. Thank you, God, for our ability to overcome hard times by relying upon Your glorious land. May others, who are not as fortunate, find happiness this Christmas. May we all feel Your presence this most important evening. Amen."

"Amen," we echoed.

And then, we ate. We ate and ate! The meal was marvelous and most of it, we had either grown or raised ourselves.

My mother made it through the whole meal. Afterward, my father carried her to the living room where they propped her in a soft chair. She looked uncomfortable and stiff, so we saved the dishes for later and went straight to the presents.

In a crazy, crowded mess, Aunt Betty handed out a similar present to each of her nephews and niece. "Here, Wally, this is yours. And Vivi, where's Vivi?" I reached up to take a small present.

We all opened our gifts at the same time. My Aunt had knitted each of us a new stocking hat and matching scarf. My set was jet black and the hat had a roll-up brim.

"That's the latest style at Heppe's," said my Aunt. On the end of the scarf were tiny glass beads that sparkled in the firelight like freshly falling snow.

"I did the beads," said Grace. I hugged her.

"Thank you, Gracie."

My Aunt had also knitted a sweater for my father and most gloriously, a woolen afghan for my mother.

"Thank you, Betty!" My mother nearly cried. "This will keep me toasty warm. It's just beautiful. It must have taken so much time."

"You're welcome, honey. I wish I could give you more."

The boys had made Uncle Al a bird house and Aunt Betty a spice rack to fit just above her oven.

"What a fine piece of craftsmanship. You could sell these in stores, you know." Aunt Betty was pleased.

And for Gracie, I gave her a skirt I had sewn myself. It was an A-line with a rose calico print and a side-zippered closure with a pearl button at the top. I'd saved for 6 months to buy the fabric, and this skirt was by far, my first sewing masterpiece.

"Oh, Vivi. It's lovely. Thank you!"

My mother whimpered, and my father needed no further warning. She cried softly as my father removed her frail body from the chair.

Somehow, I managed not to show my tears. Aunt Betty didn't try to hide hers. They streamed down her face, making wet blotches on her blue apron.

"You kids'll open your presents from your folks in the morning," she said.

We each hung our stocking by the fireplace.

"I don't know," said my father upon returning. "Santa doesn't deliver to boys who shave." He smiled at Joe Jr. and Abbott. And surprisingly, my two eldest brothers looked disappointed.

Finally, it was eleven and time to leave for church.

"So," said Uncle Al, "will the Hostadt family accompany us to Holy Hill?"

We all held our breath, watching my father wrestle with the idea of attending the Catholic Service. He avoided our stares.

"Okay," he grunted. Joe Jr. shook his head disapprovingly.

Gracie and I smiled with excitement.

We all dressed in our finest and piled into the two cars in the driveway. Uncle Al and my father drove, and Aunt Betty stayed home in case my mother needed her. With a tingling in our toes, we began the ten-mile drive to Holy Hill.

17. HOLY HILL

We drove in a ruckus, all talking and excited to be out on this cold and clear Christmas Eve. We turned onto Hwy. O and rounded a corner.

"There it is," said Uncle Al. "Nine miles to go."

Straining to see out the window, I saw the almost two hundred-foot towers of Holy Hill reaching to the sky from the top of a steep hill. They shone brilliantly within the wash of electrical lights.

"Who can win my trivia contest?" said Uncle Al. "The hill that Holy Hill sits on was carved out by…"

"Glaciers!" I shouted.

"Right, Vivian. These glaciers created thousands of hills and lakes and rivers. Who knows what our area of Wisconsin is called because of the glaciers?"

We paused, not sure.

"Bumpy?" said Walter.

We laughed.

"Yes, it's bumpy, but what's the name of our area?"

Finally, Victor muttered the answer.

"The Kettle Moraine."

"Yes!" cheered Uncle Al. "Nice job, Vic." Victor didn't take his eyes off the blackness of the window.

I imagined ice sheets covering all the land around me, and it really wasn't that hard to envision, as everywhere I looked was white.

We drove slowly, throwing out answers to Uncle Al's trivia questions. Gracie and I checked over and over to make sure my father's carload was still behind us. Finally, we curved and swerved around trees and hills and came to the entrance to Holy Hill.

"Holy Hill," said Uncle Al, remarking at hundreds of cars littering the road. We parked and began the quarter mile hike up a narrow path to the church. Uncle Al and father carried lanterns.

We entered the Shrine and I immediately fell in love with a life-sized statue of Mary.

"Look at her face," I said to Grace. She was soft-looking, her robe gently gathered and her arms open, revealing the child before her. I read the descriptive note.

"This statue was crafted in Munich, Germany and exhibited at the 1876 Philadelphia World's Fair. There, it was purchased for Holy Hill and arrived here in 1878."

As we entered the parish, we were each handed a lighted candle, and we found our seats. Soon, hundreds of candles provided our light, and the stained glass windows surrounding us sparkled with dancing colors.

I looked for my father and Joe Jr., but they were nowhere to be found.

"Where's Father?" I whispered to Uncle Al.

"In the back," he said.

"Why?"

"He thought it was better back there."

"Is Joe Jr. with him?

"Mmm."

I looked for Victor. He was behind me. He held a candle low at his waist. His eyes flashed across the ceiling, at the windows, at the people. I wondered what he was thinking. Maybe this would help him be happier.

Before us, was a 15-foot cross. I bowed before it. To me, it didn't matter what kind of church I was in. A cross was a cross. As I read from a plaque at the bottom, this cross of white oak was the original at Holy Hill that had inspired the early missionaries in the mid 1800's.

The pews were smoothly carved, dark wood, and we slid across them. I held Gracie's hand, and we snuggled in close. An incense filled the air and tickled my nose.

Suddenly, the bell choir sang.

It came upon the midnight clear
That glorious song of old
From angels bending near the earth
To touch their harps of gold
Peace on the earth, good will to men
From heav'n's all-gracious King
The world in solemn stillness lay
To hear the angels sing

Their bells twinkled and rang. Their notes echoed in the cavernous ceilings. The music was rich and came from all sides.

I felt hope and happiness wash upon me. I immediately thought of Mother. I wished she was there too, hearing and seeing and smelling. I took it all in, so I could give her the experience later.

Here was the place to pray. Here was the place to ask for help.

"Dear God," I said under my breath, "please help her. Help her not feel the pain."

Grace squeezed my hand tighter. She hadn't heard me, but she could feel it too. We were engulfed. With candles, incense, songs and emotions. Engulfed by the smells, sights and sounds of the birth of Jesus.

I heard only bits and pieces of the homily.

"Father, Jesus Christ is our light and shines upon us on this holy night."

Yes, lots of shining. Shining everywhere. The shining distracted me.

"Let this light open our hearts to peace. Allow this light to reach and saturate us with His presence."

We sang.

Oh holy night
The stars are brightly shining
It is the night of the dear Savior's birth
Long lay the world in sin and error pining
Till he appeared and the soul felt its worth

More shining!

Candlelight glowed soft white, reaching into the darkness and opening our hearts. The stained-glass windows portrayed the life of Mary, as was appropriate as the church was dedicated to her: The Shrine of Mary, Help of Christians.

The organ began. We sang, and communion ensued.

The Father paused. He spoke of unrest. For just a moment, I came out of my spell and acknowledged the growing distress in Germany. Hitler.

"Pope Pius XI spoke of the German Reich in the Mit Brennender Sorge on March 14, 1937. From the holiness of the Vatican, he asked for a rainbow of peace. Let us pray now for that rainbow. Let us pray that the German Skies are not blackened with hatred."

We prayed.

Suddenly, a single voice filled the night air with the most purely resplendent tenor solo. "Ave Maria" consumed me, and my ears became the portals into my heart.

Ave Maria
Gratia plena
Maria, gratia plena
Maria, gratia plena
Ave, ave dominus
Dominus tecum
Benedicta tu in mulieribus
Et benedictus
Et benedictus fructus ventris
Ventris tuae, Jesus.
Ave Maria

My skin prickled and my throat tightened. This man sang with such freedom! So believing. So full of hope. I was moved and inspired to the deepest depths of my soul.

During the ride home, I sat in a car of quiet. Victor sat in the front seat and rested his elbow on the window. He stared into the darkness again. But he didn't look angry anymore. Not happy either. He just looked sad.

I thanked God for my mother and my family. I thanked Him for Jeb and our outside adventures that gave me freedom and hope. I thanked God for life.

I promised to be a better Christian.

18. CHRISTMAS MORNING

We arrived home, and Walter ran to the house. A second later he stuck his head out the door, excited and happy.

"She made it! She made the melachrino!"

Gracie and I clutched arms and ran to the warm house where Aunt Betty gave us large servings of spice cake with lemon tea. The cake was soft and hot in the center with tart, lemony icing dripping down the sides.

We ate spiritedly, and Walter called out, "I've got the coin! I found it!"

Walter had found the traditional coin of silver in the cake's crust. He would be the first to open his presents in the morning.

"Not fair," said Abbott playfully. "You found it last year, too. Makes me wonder…" Abbott shot a glance at Aunt Betty who winked.

The melachrino filled our bellies with warmth, and our fingers soon thawed on the hot mugs. It was three o'clock in the morning before the house was finally quiet.

I awoke to sounds coming from the kitchen. Had I overslept? I pulled out my father's gold pocket watch: 6:15. I was fifteen minutes late! I scooted out of bed.

"Merry Christmas, Vivian," said Aunt Betty, coming up from the cellar.

"Good morning," I said, preparing my mother's breakfast. "Merry Christmas."

"Merry Christmas," I said to my mother, kissing her forehead. I administered her shot, cleansed her bedsores and came back into the kitchen. Aunt Betty and Gracie had made pancakes and sausage, and I quickly began serving sides of applesauce and scrambled eggs. It was wonderful having help in the kitchen.

Our families ate heartily, nodding "Merry Christmas" between mouthfuls and swashes of hot coffee. For only getting three hours of sleep the night before, my family was light-hearted and happy. No grumpiness today. Not even from Victor.

With breakfast over, the boys ran to the living room for their stockings. I cleared the table with Aunt Betty and Grace.

"Stop, boys," called my father. "I think we can take the time to help the women with the dishes on Christmas morning." He winked at me. I gave him my biggest smile.

Everyone chipped in and helped with the kitchen mess. Dishes galore from the night before and now our breakfast created quite a stack for washing.

Surprising us all, the phone rang. Uncle Al answered. He only spoke for a minute, then hung up.

"Betty, there's more snow coming. It's best we leave while we can."

My heart fell to the floor.

Uncle Al, Aunt Betty and Gracie packed their things. One by one, they entered my mother's room to say their holiday good-byes. Aunt Betty came out crying and threw her arms around my father.

"Oh, Joey," she whispered. "I'm so sorry. I'm just so so sorry."

"I know, Betty. Thanks for being here and bringing us Christmas smiles."

"You're welcome, sweetie."

At their car, I hugged Gracie and cried. I didn't want them to leave! I needed them here for my aching heart to feel whole. I didn't want the Christmas feeling to be over. I couldn't bear the thought of things returning to how they were.

"Merry Christmas, Vivi," said Grace. "Thank you for the skirt. And thank you for telling me your secret." She whispered now. "You be careful up there, okay?"

I nodded and swallowed my crying deep inside. "I love you, Gracie."

"I love you, too."

I handed Grace her stocking, and she hopped into the back seat. We all waved as they pulled from the driveway, leaving behind a trail of flickering snow.

Walter snapped us out of our sadness. "Let's go empty our stockings! Last one in is a rotten goose egg!"

I smiled and choked on the goose egg in my throat. Following the racing steps of eight other legs, I ran into the house to empty my stocking.

My father called after us, "Take your stockings into your mother's room."

The stockings hung swollen and heavy.

Emptying our stockings beside Mother's bed, we found candy and fruit, swizzle sticks, chocolates and butterscotch which were eaten as fast as they were discovered.

At the bottom were oranges and fruit, fresh from the market. They were bright and smelled delightful with their citrus fragrances. I peeled an orange for my mother, and she smiled as the sharp tartness of the fruit wet her lips.

And then, the exciting part.

"I'm first!" Walter said, tearing into his present, ignoring Abbott's look of disgust. He opened a shirt and new pair of Sunday church pants.

I didn't pay him any attention. I was too excited. I had a present for my mother.

I handed it to her, the package wrapped in brown paper and tied with silver string. "It's from everyone, Mother. I put it together."

She opened it. It was a pillow which had been divided into six squares. Each square had a designated family member who had signed their name in graphite. Later, I had embroidered over it.

Next to each name, I had sewn a symbol representative of that person. My father had a cow and Walter had a peppermint candy. Joseph had a jester's hat, and I had a snowflake. Abbott was an eagle. Victor had a sun, which he had requested. I didn't think it was a good match, but I didn't fight it. Maybe he wanted it because his remarks were scathing and hot.

In the middle, I embroidered a heart with the name, Mother, inside. The "T" of mother, I embellished to be a cross. My mother stared and stared at the pillow. She clutched it tightly to her chest.

"Thank you, everyone," she said. "Thank you, Vivian, for your hard work. It's precious."

I gave my mother one of my strong, gentle hugs. "You're welcome, Mother." All the work had been worth every needle-poking, finger-stabbing second.

Each child received new socks and a shirt or pants. We also received small trinkets from the Sears catalog. There were no big presents.

I could see Victor trying to hide his disappointment from the absence of new skis. I was a little disappointed myself, in that I hadn't received my watch from Knoll's. But I understood why. It was just too expensive. And, we really did need our socks and shirts.

We had all opened our presents when my mother said, "There's one more present in the basement. It's for Vivian."

"Huh?" I said. Maybe my watch? We clamored into the basement. There, in the corner of the basement, was a very large item covered with sheets. It certainly was not a watch. When did they sneak that in here?

Everyone stared at me. I wasn't sure what to do.

"There's my skis," muttered Victor.

"That's for me?" I asked my father.

"It's yours, Vivian. Go see." He had a huge smile on his face, and I could tell he was excited about the gift.

I walked past Victor and pulled the sheet off my present. My insides lurched. I caught my breath. My knees nearly buckled from the wave of sorrow crashing into them.

It was a washing machine.

"It's electric! It's already hooked up," said my father excitedly. "It has two tubs, so washing your mother's sheets and our clothes will be easier and not take so long."

I couldn't speak, and it was hard to swallow. The air was thin, and the machine became blurry. Suddenly, I felt the need to run up the steps, out the front door and as far away as I possibly could. I truly was the woman of the house, and for Christmas, when I was fifteen, I received an electric washing machine.

"I...I," I could not find the words.

Victor fumed. I found his eyes for only a second. I felt his hatred for me. I knew what he was thinking. It was my washing machine that had kept everyone from getting what they really wanted. Instead, it had gotten them a shirt, some pants and some socks.

My new washing machine was the bold-faced print my mother was dying. They acted like she was already dead.

I hated my present. I hated my father who was still smiling. I had to do something! As distraught as I was, I couldn't smother his pride. My parents didn't have a lot of extra money. No one did.

I stared at the two-tub washing machine.

"Vivian?" said my father.

I turned to him, taking in his weather-burned face and eyes filled with love.

I ran to my father and hugged him. I stood there, hugging him, wetting his chest with my saltine sorrow. He returned my hug with a strong embrace. He thought I was the happiest girl alive.

But I was not.

I was devastated.

19. SKIING AGAIN

"The mashed potatoes are lumpy," Victor complained at dinner.

Christmas was over.

"Sorry," I said.

It was amazing that one present, one thing, could completely change how I thought about myself. I used to be indestructible. I couldn't be stopped. And yet, I had been stopped. Stopped dead in my tracks by the deliverance of a Voss LS, 2-Tub and Rinse, Electro-Safe washing machine from A. A. Schmidt and Son in Hartford.

I was trapped.

Trapped in a family that never talked of the approaching death that filled our home. All of a sudden, my washing machine had released in me all the feelings I had felt for the past year, watching my mother come closer and closer to her death. My washing machine meant my mother was not going to get better. I would be doing the laundry for a long time. A long, long time even after my mother was no longer alive.

I told myself it would be okay. But my hands shook. And my eyes burned.

Walter set a stack of plates next to my soapy water. I slipped my wet dishtowel over a knife and cut my hand.

"Ow!"

"Vivi, are you okay?" said Walter.

I felt something hot and smooth on my skin. "Get out," I said softly to Walter. I didn't have to tell him twice. He ran out of the room.

Something was coming. Something emotional I couldn't control. Blood swirled into the sink, and I watched it plummet to the bottom. Just like my mother's disinfectant. I watched the scarlet drops fall to the water's surface. Drip. Drip. Drip. Each drop hit the water and slowly sank to the bottom. They were dead.

After the dishes, I went straight to my mother's room to disinfect her. I added 30 drops of iodine to my bowl, mesmerized by their sinking and swirling that mimicked my own blood. I soaked my cloth with sunshine water. She pulled open her housecoat.

"We'll begin with your left side," I said.

I felt my throat closing, and I struggled to keep my tears inside. My mother hummed, her voice soft and smooth, clean and utterly beautiful. I helped her turn to the front, and I washed the bed sores above her tailbone. They were getting worse. I checked her feet, and two small ulcerations had formed on the top of her right foot.

"How do they look, Vivian?" my mother asked.

"Okay," I lied.

I was losing control of her disease.

I soaked another hand towel in hot water and laid it on her foot to open her vessels. I finished and rinsed her clean, then carefully tucked her back into bed.

I walked into the living room. "She's ready for you, Father," I said. My father grabbed the book he would read to her tonight and wearily left the room.

"Thanks, sweetie."

At 10:00, I opened the ice box and drew her insulin.

"Good night, Mother," I whispered at her bedside. She was asleep. "I love you smoother than butterscotch." I closed her door behind me.

Victor was not tired. He sat at the table, polishing his skis and rubbing the bottoms with paraffin wax. He babied them and stroked the wood with leather. He carefully, slowly and methodically massaged and wiped and patted them. He rubbed the same spot over and over and over until I almost grabbed them away!

At 10:45, he leaned his treasures against the front door and went upstairs to bed. He didn't say a word to me. Not even a good night or Merry Christmas. Nonetheless, I thanked God for his impeccable timing and gathered my outside clothes.

At five to eleven, I snuck to the door.

"Why thank you, Victor," I mumbled. "It was so nice of you to polish my skis."

I closed the door behind me and tiptoed to the barn door. I hid behind a post. Nobody in the kitchen window. I waited, sure my father would be there, his eyes searching for me. My head painfully pounded. The pressure mingled with an ache squeezing my heart. I darted to the end of the driveway.

Jeb wasn't there yet, and I waited ten breathless minutes before seeing a shadow walk down the hill. I shivered with anticipation.

"Hi, Vivian," he called. "Sorry I'm late. My sister was full of energy tonight, and it was hard to get out." He breathed heavily. He had run the mile to our farm.

"Victor was the same way." I forced a smile and took a deep breath. "Did you have nice Christmas?"

"I ate so much, I made myself sick. Do you ever do that? Eat so much that it hurts to move?" He laughed.

"Sometimes." I tried to laugh, but it came out as a groan instead.

We walked.

"How was your…"

"What did you…"

"Sorry," Jeb said. "You first."

"I was just wondering what you got for Christmas." I forced another smile, and Jeb watched me intently. Did he know I wasn't happy?

"Well, my sister made me this scarf. And my mom made me this matching hat. And my dad made me feed the triplets." He laughed, and I managed to fake a good one that time. "Actually, I got new razor." He chuckled. "I guess that means I'm no longer a kid. How about you?"

I took another deep breath, and we turned east into some deeply snow-filled ditches. It was much harder to walk, and we exaggerated each step in order to get our legs out of the snow. The exertion released some of the stress from my shoulders and left it behind within the sleeping snowflakes.

"My Aunt Betty and Gracie made me a hat and scarf, too. I guess that must be the thing to make this year. And I got some clothes. And, well…" I closed my eyes and felt a little sick.

"What?"

"My parents gave me an electric washing machine." I thought I might throw up.

Jeb didn't respond right away. "It'll be a lot easier now."

"Yeah, yeah, I mean, it sure was expensive. And let me tell you, Victor was not happy that my washing machine kept him from getting new skis. He was mad all day." I didn't tell Jeb that it also meant my mother was dying.

"Victor will get over it. It's more important to make things easier on you than for him to get new skis. Sometimes he acts like a baby."

I looked at Jeb, surprised. I didn't know he felt that way about my brother.

"So, no watch?" he said.

"No watch. But that's okay. It was just a silly thing." Who was I kidding?

We made it to the practice jump, and I strapped my skis to my boots. It was darker tonight and harder to see. I didn't care, though. I just wanted to go fast.

The first few times down the hill were hard.

"My skis keep sinking," I called.

"Mine too. Just keep going. We have to make new tracks."

Soon, we could really practice again. I hadn't lost a thing. I skied time after time down the hill and didn't fall once.

An hour later, I took off my skis and walked to the jump. I had nothing to lose.

"I'm going to try this today," I announced, eyeing the jump from top to bottom.

"The practice jump? You really think you're ready for that?"

"I have to start sometime."

Jeb decided he couldn't stop me. "Well, let me go down a few times to make good tracks."

Jeb climbed the jump and first smoothed the snow the best he could. Happy with the slope, he strapped on his skis and went flying. It shocked me that he flew so far, even off such a small jump. He jumped three more times and stopped next to me.

"Okay, listen carefully. You must understand the jump in order to not get hurt."

"Okay."

"There are five parts to a jump. Pretty simple. The first is the "in-run." This is the part when you're going down the slide. Your knees should be bent and your arms behind you. Try it."

I bent into an egg-like position and extended my arms behind me. I bounced up and down, getting used to it. "No problem."

Jeb chuckled. "Okay, the second part is the "take off." When you reach the bottom of the slide, you straighten your legs and push off with your feet. Actually, don't push off yet. Just coast off. When you're comfortable with coasting off, you can start putting some lift into it. Lean forward and keep your chest and head over your ski tips."

"Straighten legs, push off, keep head forward." I acted out the movements.

"But don't push off yet."

"Right."

"The third part is the "flight." You try to ride the air by keeping your skis slightly apart and your body forward. Your arms should still be at your sides. It feels different than anything you've ever felt before, and you have to promise not to panic. Keep your legs straight and don't wiggle."

"Skis apart, body forward, arms down, no wiggling. Oh, and no panicking. Yes, Sir!" I gave him a salute. I was feeling better.

Jeb shifted his weight from leg to leg, uncomfortable with this. "Okay, the next part is the "landing." It's crucial to land with your legs bent, and it's easier with one ski slightly in front of the other. If your legs are straight, you won't be able to absorb the impact of the landing."

"Got it. Land with legs bent and one ski in front of the other. Try not to land backwards."

"Ha ha. Very funny. We'll see if you land backwards."

"I won't."

"Alright, the last part is the "out-run." This is when you slowly stand up, ski to the bottom and stop. You'll be going a lot faster than usual, so do your best. Don't stand up completely. Keep your knees a little bent. If you're going to fall, try to fall to one side and protect your knees." He stopped and scratched his head. "Well, any questions?"

"Nope. I'm ready."

Jeb exhaled loudly. "Why don't you start half-way up."

"If that'll make you feel better."

I climbed a little more than half-way, and with great difficulty, put on my skis. It was a lot harder starting half-way up than at the top, because I was starting on a decline instead of on a flat platform. I stood sideways, and tried to turn my skis forward, but I lost my balance and started down on one ski.

Down I went, right off the end of the jump, and I landed on my back. I coughed and sputtered. Jeb ran to my side.

"Vivian! Are you okay?"

I stared at him from my back, my skis up in the air. At first I couldn't talk. My breath was gone, and I struggled to breathe. Finally it came, and I sucked in the polar bitterness. I looked at Jeb, and the concern in his face contorted his cheeks and lips into positions I had never seen before. He looked funny.

"I didn't wiggle," I coughed. "But I did land backwards!" I was silent for a few seconds, and then I burst into laughter.

I laughed and laughed! Jeb didn't laugh at first. Rather, he looked all around, a pout on his face, not believing I was taking my fall lightly. His hands in his pockets, he frowned and sighed so loudly, I could hear him.

I was struggling for air again, but this time because I couldn't stop laughing at the realness of it all. It was amazing! Here, something physical had happened, and I had been able to respond immediately with emotion. It was freedom!

Finally, Jeb laughed too…a little. "You know," he said, "it might be difficult positioning yourself half-way up the slide. Maybe you should start on the platform."

"Hmmm. You think so?" I punched him playfully on the arm. "Thanks, coach."

I shook the snow from my jacket and climbed up the jump again. I could see Jeb pacing back and forth at the bottom. "You're making me nervous!" I called.

"You're making me nervous!" he called back.

I got to the top, and it was a hundred percent easier getting myself situated. I stood with my ski tips pointed over the edge like I'd seen the boys do on the big one. It was time. Time to prove that girls do jump.

I don't know how long I stood there, but it was a long time. I just couldn't make myself go. My mind flashed back to my day, and the thought of the washing machine made my knees weak. I saw my mother's frail body. I smelled the iodine. I watched my blood sink. I felt Victor's cold stare. I closed my eyes and wished to stay on the top of this jump forever. But I knew I couldn't. This was it. It was now or never. I had to go.

I leaned forward, bent my knees and dropped my arms to my sides. And then, I was off! I picked up speed and gasped as the icy air clawed my face while I raced down the slide. I struggled to keep my balance and reminded myself just in time to stay low and bend my knees. With my form recomposed, I reached the take off and coasted into the air.

And then I flew! I flew through the air like a bird! On wooden wings! Somehow, from deep inside, I didn't lose my form, or even wiggle. I approached the snow, and I bent my knees, landing on my right foot and then my left. I had done it!

I must have straightened my legs too much. I hit a small bump, and my body could not absorb the shock at the speed I was going. I lost my balance and headed for the snow. Quickly, I tucked into a ball and crashed to my right side.

I rolled and bounced, holding onto my legs for dear life with the fear that my knees would twist and rip. My face crashed into something sharp, and my head jerked backward. On the recoil, my face plowed into the snow, and I came to a jagged stop.

At first I just lay there, Jeb yelling something behind me. I groaned and slowly moved my legs.

I wiped snow from my face. I scraped snow from my neck. I was in pain, especially my cheek. It burned and screamed with blood and ice.

Again, my mind flashed back to the washing machine and my mother's bed sores and her bones that almost stuck right out through her thin skin. Life was so fragile. So delicate. And here I was pushing mine to the limit, risking everything for some semblance of feeling and expression of my pain.

Well, here it was, pain at its finest.

I felt my throat tightening all over again. Those tears that I had held back for so long. They were here, and there was no stopping them. They were suffocating me and killing me with their weight...the weight and burden of my mother's impending death.

My chest struggled heavily with snow-laden grief, and I started to cry. My tears wanted freedom, too.

Jeb sprinted to my side and bent down beside me. "Vivian! Oh my God, Vivian! Are you okay? Please say you're okay."

"I'm okay," I wept. "I'm okay."

I sobbed, pressing down into white fluff, grabbing for anything that could give me stability from the sinking snow that was devouring me. I was drowning in snow.

Jeb untwisted my legs and took off my skis. I sat up and leaned forward, my face in my snow-covered hands. I felt Jeb's arm around me, but there was no consolation. I cried for my mother. I cried for my family. I cried because I knew I would soon be the only girl on our farm.

Finally, I stopped. My head hung low and limp, and I kept my eyes closed. My hair hung in snow-laden clumps and formed drips down my skin where it was touching.

"Vivian, where are you hurt?" Jeb whispered.

"It's my mother," I declared for the first time ever into the open air and moonlight. "She's dying." My voice wavered in pitch and somehow, that statement released an anger in me that I wanted the world to hear. "She's dying!" I screamed.

I cried out again. "She's so sick! She's just skin and bone!"

I wept in Jeb's arms and rested my head against his chest. Finally, I had someone to listen. Someone to confide in. Finally, someone else knew what I knew. My mother wouldn't make it much longer.

Jeb helped me home. He carried my skis and guided me through drifts. It was 2:30 in the morning when we got to my house. We hid behind the corner of the barn, wary that someone may be watching. Haydie stood perfectly still and watched us

Jeb could see my cheek by the light. "You're going to be black and blue tomorrow. What will you say?"

I shook my head. "I'll think of something."

"Will you be okay, Vivian?"

"I'll be okay."

He leaned forward and kissed me for the second time, this time on my lips. He lingered for a moment, and I felt that snowball come back.

"If you need anything, you ask me," he said, holding my shoulders. "I'll do anything you ask."

I nodded. "Good night."

I snuck into the house. I didn't bother to take off my jacket and boots and snow pants, rather went straight to work. I found a scrap piece of leather, and I rubbed and rubbed Victor's skis with paraffin wax until they gleamed and glistened in the firelight like a newly fallen snow. I leaned them against the door, re-stocked the fires, peeled off my clothes and crawled into bed.

As I lay there, my head pulsed and my cheek stung. I wracked my brain for an excuse for such an injury, but I didn't think of one before I fell asleep. I didn't dream, rather sunk into the deepest sleep I'd had in months.

I was perfectly still, and didn't even flinch until I heard voices in the kitchen.

20. BLACK AND BLUE

"Jeb was right," I whispered, looking into the mirror.

I was bloody and as blue as Turtle Lake in July when I awoke. I winced from the soreness of my back and right side. The boys had left for the barn, and I soaked a towel in hot water from the stove reservoir. I started my mother's eggs cooking and placed the towel to my cheek to soak off the crusted blood. The heat felt good.

I looked in a mirror. The scratch itself wasn't deep. It was the discoloration that stood out. Dark red, blue and purple covered my cheekbone and spread all the way back to my hairline. I looked as if I had been beaten.

I gently retrieved my mother's morning shot, bending stiffly and supporting my ribs and back by bending only my knees and not my waist. I toasted her bread. When I entered her room, she must have sensed something was wrong by my lateness, because she noticed my cheek immediately.

"Vivian! What happened?" She was sitting, and struggled to get a better look.

I toned it down. "Hmm? Oh, my cheek? It's okay. I just fell, that's all."

"When did you fall between last night and this morning?"

"I tripped when I loaded the furnaces last night. I fell right into the wood stack and smacked my cheek on a piece of firewood." I could lie good under pressure.

"It looks terrible, Vivi. Maybe you should put something cold on it."

"It's okay, Mother. I have your shot here." I began my process of making sunshine water, and my mother leaned her head against the headboard. She watched me.

"You have a lot on your shoulders, Vivian," she said. I stopped, but didn't look at her. "I'm sorry to have placed this burden on you."

I felt like a wretch. I sat on her bed and took her hand. "No, Mama. I just want to take care of you. That's all that matters."

"And you've taken wonderful care of me, dear. You have managed my medicines and kept me from getting infections. I think you will help many people someday. It is in your heart to help people."

"Yes, Mother. Did you know I want to become a doctor?" There, she was now the second person to know my dream.

"A doctor? Really?" She paused for a moment, thinking it through, and I hoped she didn't doubt me. "Honey, someday you will be a remarkable doctor. You're smart and driven and filled with love."

I hugged my mother, and it was now official. I would become a doctor. My mother knew my dream and believed I could do it, and I wouldn't let her down...whether she was alive or not.

My Christmas blues were over. My mother and Jeb had mended me. And perhaps, I had healed myself by releasing my tears.

The morning passed quickly, and I focused on mid-week laundry and trying to avoid any sudden movements that sent piercing pain into my side, back and shoulder. I used my electric washer for the first time, and as much as it had hurt me in the beginning, my laundry time was cut by more than half. My life would be easier because of it. I would have to thank my father and mother more sincerely.

At two o'clock, I found myself uncharacteristically with nothing immediate to do, and I snuck into my bed to lie down. I wrapped the heavy, woolen blankets over my broken body and let the mattress envelope me with its softness. I drifted into a deep sleep and awoke at four o'clock, feeling more alert, but stiff. I gave my mother her shot and snack and started dinner.

Just before the boys came in, I checked my rock for messages. To my surprise, there were two! My stomach lurched as I realized the possibility that somebody had discovered my secret. Why hadn't I thought of that?

The first note I opened was from Rosemary.

Merry Christmas, Vivian!
Christmas was splendid at my house. How about you? I received two new dresses and a gorgeous watch from Knoll's. You will love it.

I nodded my head with irony. Rosemary, the daughter of the owners of Heppe's Department Store, had gotten my watch for Christmas. It figured.

Did you hear about the dance at the Schwartz?? You have to go! I'm wearing my new gown from St. Nick. It's red and drop-dead beautiful. Just wait till Victor sees me. Did I tell you I'm planning on marrying Victor now? What better way for us to be real sisters!
Have you talked to Jeb lately? I haven't seen him. I miss you and can't wait to talk to you about the dance!
Love,
Rosie

I gasped when I saw what was written next. In what seemed to be coal, she had scribbled,

Who is J?

I opened Jeb's note.

Meet you at 11. —J

I stood there, in drifts of snow, holding the notes in my hands. My two worlds were colliding! Crashing into each other with punches and kicks. My fiery cheek and pulsing headache reminded me of my inability to hide my secret, and I wondered if Jeb and I should continue. It was getting more and more dangerous.

"I have to talk to Rosemary," I said to myself. If I didn't get to her soon, she would talk. Rosemary liked to talk.

I could just see it. Rosemary talking to the boys and girls at the diner in town about Vivian's secret note. Who was it from? Why were they meeting? It was the perfect kind of winter gossip and distraction that would get the whole town talking and forgetting about the two drab and drearily cold months to come.

I walked briskly back to our house, the wind biting my raw skin and the arctic sting freezing my nose.

Pork chops, canned beans and biscuits filled our table at dinnertime and most everybody kept to themselves. I did too, my mind filled with thoughts of skiing and notes, Rosemary and gossip, dresses, dances and Jeb. I should just ask them, I thought. Ask them about the dance. But, I was so paranoid about anyone finding out about Jeb that I didn't. I would be patient and wait.

After dinner, I speed-washed the dishes and sat at the table to hear my father read the Hartford Times Press. Sure enough, the dance was big news, and he read about it on the second page.

"President Honored Through Efforts to Plan Fourth Annual Nation-Wide Ball for Infantile Paralysis."

I held my breath.

"As our President's birthday falls on January 30th, so will our fourth national Infantile Paralysis Ball in his honor. Led by national Chairman of the Ball, Colonel Henry L. Doherty, over 5,000 nation-wide communities will contribute to this event, each holding marvelous dances in their own respective towns."

"Motion picture stars, radio celebrities and local heroes are coming together to make this year's fund raiser the brightest and most profitable yet."

"Hartford will host its ball at the marvelous Schwartz Park Pavilion on January 30. A source of pride for Hartford, the octagonal ballroom was completed in the late 1920's and is a prominent Midwestern landmark known for hosting brilliant musicians and performers. Music will be provided by the swing-stepping "Pep" Babler and his Dance Orchestra. Tickets will go on sale January 10, 1938."

There it was. I desperately wanted to go to the dance with Jeb. I thought of Rosemary in her new ball gown and couldn't believe that of all people, she wanted to go with Victor. Maybe I could get a new dress, too. Just the thought of shopping for a new dress was exciting. Maybe if I counted all my money…

My father began summarizing the 1937 Wisconsin Legislative Movements when I gingerly departed to disinfect my mother. I'd heard what I needed to.

My mother was still picking at her dinner when I entered her room. Abbott left to attend the nightly reading, and I opened the iodine. My mother did not look well. Her face was ghostly white, and her breathing, slow.

"Mother, you didn't eat your dinner."

"No, dear, I'm just not hungry tonight."

I knew the complications of such a dilemma. "But Mother, if you don't eat, your insulin will move all your sugar out of your blood and you'll be low."

"I know, Vivian. Don't worry, I've eaten enough to prevent that." I looked at her plate and determined that she had eaten four, maybe five bites.

"Maybe for now, but not later. What would you like better? Some toast? Applesauce?"

"No, dear, I'm fine."

"No, Mother, you are not fine! You need to eat more."

I left her room and stomped back through jolts of rib pain with a nice-sized portion of applesauce I had made myself. Just a touch of cinnamon. My mother picked at it, and by the time I had finished her nightly cleaning, she'd finished it all. I felt better.

We sat and talked. I told her about the ball, and it was quite clear I wanted to go.

"Who will you go with?" she asked. Her eyes instantly tightened on me, gripping me, waiting for my answer.

"Well, I'm not sure yet."

"Maybe Jeb?"

"Maybe." I couldn't hide it any longer. "He and I have been talking a lot lately."

"You have?"

"Mmmm. He's very nice."

"Handsome too. Quite a dreamboat." My mother laughed softly, and I had to agree. Jeb was dreamy.

My father came in, and I finished my kitchen duties while he and my mother read and snuggled. Soon, it was almost eleven, and I gathered Victor's skis.

Jeb was there. Waiting for me just like he said he would be. He was as reliable as my father's pocket watch.

"Hi, Vivian." He inspected my cheek. "Oof. How'd you pull that one off?"

"It wasn't hard, really. I just told everyone I had a vicious encounter with a piece of firewood. It's dark when I stoke the fires at night, so it wasn't hard to sell."

"Does it hurt?"

"Naw." I stopped. I could be honest with Jeb. "Actually, it hurts a lot, but it's my side that bothers me the most. But, I can ski."

"So, you're okay? I mean, really?" He wasn't talking about my cheek. Jeb searched my face for clues.

I smiled at his concern. "I'm better."

Jeb took my skis, and we walked together to the practice jump. I moved slowly, gingerly, protecting my sore torso as we went.

"You know, I was thinking," he said. "Maybe we shouldn't be doing this. It's dangerous, and I don't want you to get hurt, more than you already are."

Jeb's jaw-line was tight. I blocked the pain that wracked my body. I breathed deeply, walking smoothly without any limp. I had to convince him otherwise.

"I've thought about it too. But, I can't stop. I have to keep jumping. If I don't, I don't know how I'll make it through the winter."

Jeb's eyes were big and round. "You're going to jump off the big one, aren't you?" I looked into his worry-filled face, and my heart warmed.

"Yes," I said.

It was just that easy. I would jump off the big one.

Jeb nodded his head. He had known it all along. "Well, okay, then I guess the only thing I can do is make sure I teach you right and we practice a lot before you try it. Let's go." He walked faster and excitement whisked me forward.

He was in.

I'm not sure how I did it with my bumps and bruises, but I worked on my downhill skiing and stopping for some time before attempting the practice jump again. Somehow, I managed to not fall as badly as the last time.

I jumped six times, each time my body becoming more accustomed to the feel of gravity pulling me through the air and my skis hitting the ground in a wave of spraying snow. Each time I jumped, I improved, and by the end of the night, Jeb's posture had softened. He was becoming more comfortable with the idea of it...the big one. I could see it. And it was only because of one reason.

I was a natural.

21. A PRESENT FOR ME

During the next three weeks, and for the first time in a year, I was thankful for no school. I kept up with my chores easily and napped in the afternoons. Because of this, I could see Jeb at night. Our outings were mostly limited by moonlight. We could jump with very little, but with nothing, we were sunk. Lucky for me, most nights were clear.

One night, I returned from skiing so tired, I was almost asleep before I hit my pillow. Victor carried his skis down to the kitchen the next morning.

"Walter, have you been playing with my skis?" Victor asked. I gasped at the sink.

"Uh uh," said Walter. He continued playing with his truck.

"You better not be lying to me. I can see they're all scuffed up."

I clanged my pots together, trying to draw their attention away from the skis.

"Uh uh," said Walter.

Victor grabbed Walter's shirt. "You better not touch 'em again, or I'll scuff you up, too."

Victor's anger frightened me. My mind raced.

"So, did you do it?" Victor didn't stop. "Tell me!"

Walter's eyes bulged. He didn't fight back or try to defend himself.

I took a deep breath. I had to tell him the truth. "Victor, I..."

"What's going on?" Joe Jr. asked, walking into the room.

Victor pushed Walter to the floor. "Nothing. This has been resolved." He grabbed his jacket and headed for the barn.

"You okay, Wally?" said Joseph.

"Uh huh," said Walter. He looked at me, and ran up the stairs.

"Don't let that jerk push you around, Wal," Joseph called up to Walter. "He's just an old grouch."

Walter didn't answer.

1938 started with runs down the ski jump and falls too, but none as bad as my first. The bruising on my cheek faded from blue to green to a dull brownish-yellow. My soreness was replaced by an increase in my stamina. I was getting stronger. I lived for my night-time adventures, counting down the chores and shots until 11:00.

"I can't believe school starts again in five days," said Walter sadly. "I don't want it to."

"Me too," I said, surprised with myself.

I finished my last load of laundry and hung my mother's sheets on the basement lines to dry. With supper already prepared, I took my afternoon nap and spent extra time with my mother.

"So, has Jeb asked you to the dance yet?" she said.

My heart lunged from my chest. "Nope, not yet."

"Maybe he'll ask you at school on Monday."

"Maybe." I had more hoped he would ask tonight. I'd have to check my rock to make sure we were meeting, but I had no reason to believe we wouldn't. I wasn't sure how Jeb did it. He never seemed to be tired, and I didn't know if he had time to nap. Nonetheless, there was usually a note waiting for me under my rock, and Jeb was never more than ten minutes late from meeting me at 11.

"If he does ask you, what will you wear?"

I sat at my mother's bedside, knitting a scarf and not sure I wanted her to see my desire for a new dress. "I don't know. Maybe Rosemary will let me borrow a dress of hers." Not likely. Rosemary did not like to share. "Anyway, he has to ask me first."

At dinnertime, I served my boys chicken, sweet potatoes, cinnamon bread and baked apples. Walter gave me his nod of approval for my sweetened dinner, and I had to admit, I'd sweetened it up just for him. Perhaps out of guilt for Victor's bullying.

With dinner over, I went to the barn to feed Haydie. She crazily attacked my pan, and I ran to my rock as quickly as I could. As expected, I found a note waiting for me.

See you at 11. –J

I disinfected my mother and rinsed her clean. Her bed sores had grown smaller with extra care, and the ulcerations on her right foot had almost healed. It was taking a long time, but with moist, hot towels on her feet almost every daylight hour, her circulation had allowed the healing process to resume. Dr. Winston was amazed.

"Really, Vivian," he'd said, "your mother has had an extended life because of you. You should be very proud."

But I wasn't proud. Just desperate.

My father talked with my mother until ten o'clock, and I administered her shot. As I left the room she said, "Good night, Vivian. I love you more colorful than a prairie of Wisconsin wildflowers."

"Good night, Mother. I love you sweeter than Ghirardelli chocolate."

"Mmmm," my mother sighed, "that's a lot of love."

At 11:00, I met Jeb. I was shocked to see he didn't have his skis.

"Is everything okay?" I said.

"Yeah, everything's fine. I thought maybe we could just talk tonight."

Talk? Something was wrong. My heart sunk that I wouldn't get to ski, but then again, the intrigue of listening to Jeb "just talk" overwhelmed me.

"Come on." I took him by the hand and led him to the hay loft. Inside, I scrounged up some woolen horse blankets, and we burrowed into the cold hay. It was freezing at first, but we snuggled, held each other and warmed quickly, together. I liked "just talking."

We lay there until even my toes were warm. Jeb brushed the hair from my face and smiled.

"What is going on here?" I said.

"I have something for you."

I moved closer. "What?"

Jeb reached into his jacket pocket and took out a small box wrapped in brown paper. It was tied with a simple piece of twine. "Merry Christmas," he said.

"Jeb!"

"I know it's way past Christmas, but I've been saving money, and then there was this sale, and well, Merry Christmas." It was the biggest smile I'd ever seen on him.

I took the box. My stomach turned in spiraling circles and twinged into jumps and belly flops as I untied the string. I opened the paper carefully and took out the box. On the top of the box was a gold, glittering emblem that said, Knoll's. I giggled. Jeb placed his hand on my knee, and I opened my treasure. There, was my watch.

Within the safety of the barn, I squealed and jumped into Jeb's arms. "Thank you! Thank you, Jeb!"

I hugged him and kissed him and stared at my watch. It was silver, shiny and delicate, and glistened like silvery snowflakes. And, it was fragile, like a lady's watch should be. The face was so small, and the numbers, fancy and swirling. I held it to my ear and the faint tick tick tick lulled my heart like a lullaby. It was beautiful.

"So, do you like it?" he asked.

I laughed out loud. "Do I like it? I…I…"

Gently, Jeb took the watch from me and latched it to my wrist. His hands were big and callused compared to the tininess of the watch, and my soul melted with the loveliness of it all. I loved my watch. I loved Jeb.

"It's the nicest present anyone has ever given me."

"I have something to ask you, Vivian," Jeb said.

My insides flipped. No wonder why he didn't want to ski.

"Yes?"

"Well, I'd really like to take you to the…"

"Yes!" I didn't give him time to go any further. "I'd love to go to the dance!"

"Well, just wait. There's one big problem." Jeb's smile turned into a frown.

"What? What is it?"

"I can't really dance, though," he said. At that moment, I thought he was the cutest boy alive.

"That's okay. I don't really know how to dance either. And anyway, if we can hurtle down a ski jump and fly through the air together, we certainly can dance together. You just have to promise me not to panic. And, no wiggling." He snickered, we kissed, and the time passed even more quickly than a jumping night.

Soon enough, Jeb left, and I found myself tucked in bed listening to my new watch. The tick tick tick resonated with hope and trust and symbolized my entire belief in Jeb. He was my rock. My center. I couldn't wait to dance with him. Even if we spent the entire night stepping on each other's feet or tripping in front of the whole town.

I wondered if any other girls in the world had ever had a boy do such wonderful things for them as Jeb had done for me. I thanked God for my mother, warm, sweet hay and even itchy, smelly horse blankets. I thanked God that I was alive and in my bed listening to the tick tick tick of my new watch. I thanked God for Jeb.

In my dreams, I dreamt of carriages, princesses, castles and a prince. The prince twirled his partner around and around beneath a crystal chandelier. And as the prince spun his princess, it was clear his girl was me.

22. BLACK SATIN

Saturday went like any other Saturday, except much easier. I had already made my week's supply of bread, and doing the laundry was so quick now with my electric washer, I sometimes couldn't believe the free time on my hands.

Victor spent his morning in the hay stack while my father, Joe Jr., Abbot and Walter went into the woods, cutting firewood for our hot, hungry furnaces. Freshly chopped wood was harder to get started, but once it was, it burned hotter and longer.

The men were cold, sweaty and tired when they got home, and my brothers gobbled their grilled cheese sandwiches and slurped their tomato soup ravenously before scooting to the barn to start the afternoon chores.

I opened the ice box and removed my mother's shot. I took it to her room.

"How are you feeling?"

I removed a cool towel from her foot and replaced the towel with a hot one. Still no signs of infection.

"I'm fine, Vivian." She pulled open her housecoat, and I held my breath as I gave the medicine. "I have something for you to see," she said.

She motioned to a large box on the table beside her closet. It was open, but whatever was inside, had not yet been removed. I tipped one side of the box and dust swirled upward, forming clouds in her electric light. This box had not been opened for some time.

"What is it?" I said.

"Why don't you look?" my mother beamed.

My curiosity skated in speedy figure-eights, and peeling away layers of brittle paper, and pushing aside mothballs, I lifted out the most majestic gown I had ever seen.

"What is this?" I asked in shock.

"That is the dress I wore when I was the 'Queen of Christmas,'" my mother explained. "Every year when I was growing up, a local girl was chosen as the Queen of the winter holidays. When I was fifteen, I was queen. My Grandmother Re made that dress for me. It's black satin. It's only been worn once."

I glided my finger down the fabric. It was dense, cool and smooth. The richness of the black material shone metallic silver in certain rays of light, enhancing the color and illustrating the elegance that had only been displayed once for the world to see.

I turned the dress and saw a perfect feature. Across the bodice, and following gathered darts for a snug fit, were tiny glass beads in the shapes of snowflakes. They glistened and sparkled in my mother's electric light and were almost a perfect match for the hat and scarf that Aunt Betty and Gracie had made for me for Christmas. They reminded me of Jeb.

"You never told me you were a queen," I said mischievously.

I imagined her dark hair and deep brown eyes twinkling amidst the translucent beads. I could visualize the defined line of black satin meeting pale, Sicilian skin.

My mother watched me. "I don't know if it's something you would want to wear to the ball with Jeb, but if you like it, you may have it."

"Mother, I've never seen something so beautiful!"

"Why don't you try it on?"

I didn't waste a second. I stripped down to my thermals and slipped the moth-ball smelling dress over my head. I felt the cool, smooth satin against my neck as it softly and delicately fell into place.

My mother fastened the back hooks, and the bodice fit me perfectly. A scooped neckline in the front reached up to the outermost corners of my shoulders where the sleeves gently rested, perfectly balanced upon the tips of my collarbones. The sleeves were long, thin and tight, all the way to my wrists, where tiny little slits allowed my hands to sneak through. The bodice reached down to my waist where the dress softly opened at my hips into a fullness that only a queen had known before me. The satin was thick, silky, soft and so dark, I could only compare it to a night sky with no moon.

I stood in front of a mirror and was dead silent. I couldn't believe what I was seeing. I remembered pictures of my mother from her youth. And here she was, looking back at me from the mirror's reflection.

I looked just like my mother.

"Vivian," my mother said, "you are absolutely beautiful."

I ran to my mother's bedside and hugged her, stepping on the hem of my dress that would have to be shortened.

"Thank you, Mother! Thank you for letting me wear your dress."

"It's your dress now," she said. "You may have it, if you promise me one thing."

I nodded.

"When you get back from the dance, I want to hear everything. I want to hear about the Schwartz and the decorations and the people and the dresses and the band. I want to see the dancing and smell the pipe tobacco. I want to hear it all."

"I promise. I'll tell you everything."

It was late, and I hung my gown in the basement to air out. I went upstairs and made Walter's favorite side-dish. I received my anticipated nod from my youngest brother and watched as he helped himself to four spoonfuls of carrot pudding.

I felt whole. I felt appreciated. Tonight was a night unlike many others I had experienced in the past year. I felt like the world was turning and time was passing exactly how it should be.

I finished my nightly duties.

"Good night, Vivian. I love you stinkier than mothballs," my mother laughed.

"Good night, Mother. I love you smoother than black satin."

"Ahhh. That's a lot of love."

In bed, slowly breathing, I closed my eyes and listened...*tick tick tick*.

23. HARD TO WATCH

Sunday morning, I finished my chores just in time for my father to see me.

"Vivian, are you done with your chores?" he asked.

"Yes, Father," I answered. I picked up my jacket, ready to go to the ski hill.

"Great, I'll meet you at the car for church."

It was not what I had planned! I'd planned on going to the ski hill and watching the boys get ready. I had planned on meeting Jeb there the second he arrived. I'd planned on seeing Rosemary and talking to her about the note. But instead, I climbed into the Model A Ford with Victor and Walter, and we headed for St. Olaf's. I didn't think it was what Victor had planned either.

Later, back at home, I gave my mother her ten o'clock shot and snack.

"I'll be back at two." I checked my watch, and it was right on. I wouldn't be late this time.

Victor and I could have walked to the ski hill together, as we left only seconds apart, but instead he walked in front of me, increasing the gap between us with each over-exaggerated step. He carried his skis on his shoulder, and I was jealous! Those were my skis! By the time we got to the hill, he was so far in front of me, I couldn't find him.

The crowd was big, with people milling in and out of stands and trees.

"Vivian! Over here!"

Rosemary's face was flushed, and her pink cheeks offset the darkness of her hair with a new, snow-white beret.

"Hi, Rosie! Hi, Anita Mae!" I gave my girlfriends a hug, and we chattered. I saw Rosemary's watch and wasn't surprised to see that her watch from Knoll's was studded with diamonds. I showed her mine.

"That's nice, Vivi," she said.

"Thanks. Jeb gave it to me. It was exactly the one I'd wished for."

Rosemary and Anita Mae's eyes grew round, and suddenly my watch was much more interesting.

"So, are you and "J" going steady?" Rosemary emphasized the "J" and I caught my breath, knowing she was referring to the note. I smiled at her, downplaying her attempt to shake me up.

"Yeah, I think so. We've never said it like that, but sometimes, we meet and talk after my mother's mid-morning shot. But not often. He works on the farm, you know."

There! I had explained the note with a tiny lie. She didn't know that eleven o'clock was at night. Now she thought we met during the day.

"Wow, Vivian," said Anita Mae. "Are you and he going to the dance?"

"Yes, and I even have my dress."

"Wait 'til you see my dress. It's red with a low-cut neckline and lots of ruffles that flap up around my knees when I move." Rosemary grabbed the sides of her woolen coat and flapped them into the air. "The boys will love it!" she tossed her hair to the other shoulder. "Whom is Victor going with?"

"No one, yet."

"Well, I'm giving him until tomorrow. If he doesn't ask me by then, I'm going to have to go with someone else. I can't wait forever. All the good boys will be taken."

Just then, Jeb caught my eye, and he waved to me from the top of the esker. I waved back.

"Look," said Rosemary, "it's Mr. Skalstad!"

Mr. Skalstad made his way to the top of the jump for the test run. He stepped forward, the tips of his skis dangerously hanging over the platform of the jump. He leaned forward, his arms at his sides. And he was off!

I watched him descend down the jump and found the experience to be different than in the past. I watched his in-run and noted that he kept his legs bent and arms slightly back. He pushed off hard at the take off and shot into the air, straightening his legs and keeping his chest and head over his ski tips. He landed in perfect form, with one ski slightly in front of the other. He skied to the bottom, swerving side-to-side and stopped in a brilliant display of spraying snow. He had executed a perfect jump.

Rosemary squealed and cheered, idolizing Erv's father. Anita Mae stayed quiet as usual, and I wanted desperately to leave my girlfriends to join the boys at the top. I could almost feel Victor's skis attached to my feet. It was agonizing to watch them each take their turn shooting off the end of the ski jump, racing down the hill. I wanted to jump!

I stayed with the girls all morning and early afternoon. I cheered for Jeb and admired Victor's improvement from the last time.

"He's getting better, Vivian," said Rosemary, her eyes narrowed.

"Yes, smoother and his landing was even. He didn't push off, though."

Rosemary and Anita looked at me strangely. I was no longer just an observer. I was a critic.

The hours passed quickly, and I checked my watch often as 2:00 approached at lightning speed. With 25 minutes to spare, I found Jeb and told him I had to go home.

"Will I see you tonight?" I asked. "If you're not too tired, I'd really like to ski tonight." I hoped he would say yes, although I knew that if he didn't, I would see him tomorrow at school.

"Yeah, sure. I think I can manage to schedule you in, Miss Vivian."

We hid behind an evergreen. Jeb smiled and wrapped his arms around my waist.

"It's hard to watch and not be one of the skiers," I whispered.

"I bet. I kept expecting you to tackle Victor and put the skis on in his place."

"Hmmm. Not a bad idea. Maybe next time."

Jeb kissed me tenderly good-bye.

"I'll see you 11:00," he called, checking over his shoulder to see if anyone heard.

I turned and waved. "Eleven, it is."

I couldn't help but laugh as I walked away. Because this time, I knew a secret. I wasn't going to practice on the practice jump tonight.

I was going down the big one.

24. CONTROL

I gave my mother her shot right on time. I stroked the smooth face of my watch and cooked dinner. Rice, beef stroganoff and beans cooked for two hours while I made fresh cinnamon rolls. The boys came in hungry, and I listened to the excitement.

"Did you see Erv's last jump?" said Victor. He was more talkative than usual. Definitely in his element.

"Yeah, he's tough," said Abbot. "Think he can beat Halverson at the tourney?"

"It'll be close, but he'll do it."

"I still think you should beat 'em both and take the new skis for yourself," said Joe Jr.

"In my dreams," Victor scoffed. "On my best day, maybe I could take Erwin on his worst day. But beat Erv and Halverson on the same day? No way."

"You just need to work on your take off," I said.

I immediately regretted it. The boys stared at me. My father even stopped eating.

"What?" Victor demanded.

"Ahem!" I cleared my throat. "I mean, I don't know. I just was watching today, and I noticed that Mr. Skalstad really pushed off when he jumped into the air. I thought, maybe if you pushed off more, you'd go further. You know, physics."

I busied myself, pushing my stroganoff away from my beans, then back together, studying it on my fork, making a letter J with it and eating it like it was the best gourmet food ever made. My brothers were perfectly silent. I pretended nothing was wrong. Finally, they went on like nothing had been said.

"Ask Rosemary Heppe to the dance yet?" Joe Jr. asked Victor. Victor's face turned bright red. "You'd better ask her soon, or I might ask her myself."

"You better not," said Victor. He really was interested in Rosemary.

"She's not going to wait around for you forever, Victor," I added. Victor shot me a well-practiced look of hatred.

The rest of the meal was quiet, except for the loud food-smacking when Walter devoured three of my cinnamon rolls. He nodded in my direction, and I flashed him a smile. We had an understanding, Walter and I. It was unspoken, but there.

After dinner, I cleaned the dishes and listened to fifteen minutes of my father's after-dinner lesson. I exited to disinfect my mother. We talked of dances.

Mother groaned and tensed as I rolled her to her front. We stopped talking, and I concentrated on being gentler. I finished rinsing her from head to toe, and placed a hot towel on her foot. I left as Victor came in to read to her while my father checked a cow we were expecting to freshen. The labor was just starting.

"I'll be back at 10," I said. Mother smiled. Victor didn't even look at me. "See ya, Victor," I pressed my luck. Of course, he didn't answer.

At ten, I gave my mother the last of her shots and tucked her into bed. I couldn't wait to get to the ski hill. I'd had a good night.

"Goodnight, Vivian. I love you fresher than a spring rain."

"Goodnight, Mother. I love you more fragrant than roses."

"Mmmm. That's a lot of love."

I met Jeb at 11:00.

"Let's go this way tonight," I said, leading him away from our normal path and toward the trail that led to the big hill. He stopped.

"What are you doing, Vivian?" he said. His tone surprised me.

"Well," I squirmed, "after watching the boys today, I thought maybe I could start on the big one."

"You're not ready."

"I think I am! I've been practicing on the small one for weeks, and I'm comfortable with it now."

"You're going to kill yourself. And I'm not going to help you."

It was time to compromise. If I pushed too far, Jeb would leave altogether.

"Okay. You're right. I'm not ready to jump, but I am ready to start practicing skiing down the esker. I have to be able to ski down a steeper hill and stop first, right? Can't we just do that tonight?" I took Jeb's hand and squeezed it. "Please?"

He did one of his noisy sighs and gave in. "Okay. But only downhill. No jumping off the big one until I say you're ready."

"Okay." I started to walk, but stopped when Jeb stayed put.

"Really, Vivian. You have to promise me. You won't jump off the big one until I say you're ready."

I had two choices. I could promise and put my jumping in his control. Or, I could deny the promise and take many steps back, probably making Jeb angry in the process. I chose to move forward.

"I promise."

"Thank you, Vivian."

We made it to the top of the esker, and I put on my skis. I took them off, though, to walk halfway down and try from mid-way. I just couldn't make myself start from the top without giving halfway a trial run first.

I did alright! I skied to the bottom faster than ever before and came to an ungraceful stop, plowing into Victor's straw bales. Like brother, like sister. Crash 1 and Crash 2.

For the rest of the evening, I skied half-way. I reached the bottom at racing speeds, and only fell half the time. I considered it a success.

Jeb walked me home, and we talked of the school day that would start in a little more than five hours.

"I won't be able to ski as much now that school is starting," Jeb said.

I nodded. "I know. It's too hard."

"I get tired. And when I'm tired, I can't do my studies. I have to get good grades if I'm going to get accepted to law school."

"And me too if I'm going to become a doctor." Reality choked me. I wasn't going to ski as much anymore.

"We'll still go once or twice a week, though." Jeb kissed my forehead. "Don't worry, Vivian. I won't let you stop jumping."

I smiled at my favorite boy in the whole world. "I don't want to."

"I know. I'll see you at school tomorrow."

Jeb left.

I quietly entered the house. I set Victor's skis on the kitchen table, and it wasn't until I was wiping them with a towel, that I noticed Walter standing in the hallway.

"Walter!" I whispered. "What are you doing awake?"

"I just came in from the barn," he said. "The cow had her baby." His eyes were huge. His mouth was open. He knew what I was doing was wrong, even if he didn't know exactly what I was doing.

"Where's Father?" I demanded.

"He's in the barn. With the calf. He'll be here in a minute."

I panicked. I ripped off my hat and pulled my boots off, throwing them toward the pile by the door. I had just walked past the barn with my father inside it.

"Look," I said, "sometimes I go out at night and go sledding. And sometimes I try out Victor's skis, too. Just in the drifts." I talked quickly.

Walter was motionless.

"You're not going to tell, are you?" I asked. "Are you?" I was angry with my sloppiness. "Answer me!"

Walter stood in silence, then shook his head. "I won't tell." He ran upstairs.

My heart raced as I speed-polished Victor's ski's to a less-than-perfect shine. I peeked out the kitchen window for my father, expecting him to burst through the door shouting, "Gotcha!" But, he didn't.

I tore off my outerwear and darted into bed without washing my face or changing into dry clothes. I was hot and afraid. The kitchen door opened. I held my breath.

My father came into the house, and I strained to breathe slowly and quietly as I listened to him shuffle through the kitchen.

"Please, no," I whispered. "Please, no."

He creaked up the stairs. He hadn't noticed the extra big puddles and snow on the floor. He didn't care if the skis were wet. He hadn't noticed my door was closed more than usual. He never suspected I'd been out. Hopefully, Walter wouldn't tell.

I needn't have worried, however, as Walter was true to his word. I thanked God for the one part of Walter that had nurtured his love for me in the past few months…his sweet-tooth.

25. SCHOOL RESUMES

School was dreadful.

For the first time, I didn't enjoy attending my classes and interacting with my school-mates. I found it hard to concentrate on my studies, my mind often wandering to jumping and the tick tick tick of my ladies wristwatch.

And, I was so tired.

"Vivian," said Mr. Mallory. I jumped out from a daze.

"Yes, Sir," I said.

"Maybe a trip outside with the erasers will wake you up."

"Yes, Sir," I said. I got up and gathered the erasers. It was a cold day.

I shivered as I banged the erasers together. Chalk dust floated into a powdery cloud, and my mind wandered again. I whispered, "Fresh snow."

I thought of Jeb and the big jump, the hayloft, and our itchy, smelly horse blankets. I was obsessed with the dance at the Schwartz that would take place a week from Wednesday. The ball was so big, school was to be canceled the following Thursday, so the youth of Hartford could recuperate.

I checked my rock for messages. I knew there wouldn't be any, as Jeb had said he was tired. Nonetheless, I checked. No note for me. My heart sank, and I cried right there on the bridge. The life that had felt okay to me was gone. My old one was back.

On Friday, I practiced on the big one again, climbing a little higher each time, plummeting down the steep slope of the esker only to abruptly stop myself at the bottom. I kept my body low, my knees bent and my arms back.

"Let the Earth decide whether you bend or straighten your knees," Jeb said. "You can't control the hill's surface. Your body should only respond." It was getting easier.

We skied Saturday night too, even after my extensive day of chores and more chores.

And because I was so tired, my body didn't respond right. My judgment was off. Trees became blurry, the deceiving snow reaching up at my feet, pulling me downward, trying to make me fall. At one point, I miscalculated my stopping point and crashed into a bush far left of the straw bales.

"I think we'd better go home," Jeb said. I agreed.

On Sunday, I finished my chores early in order to hem the skirt of my ball gown.

"Isn't that a bit short, Vivi?" my mother asked, looking at my handiwork.

"Maybe so," I answered, "but most girls are wearing their dresses just below their knees at school. I think it's nice."

My mother nodded, still not sure. I tried my dress on again. It was gorgeous.

Jeb and I skied Monday night, and I almost reached the top of the esker.

"I'm so close now!" I cheered jubilantly.

"Close, but not ready to jump yet," Jeb said.

I put on my tough face and tried to look as smooth as I could as I flew down. I had to convince him I had control of my descent.

As the day of the ball approached, I grew more excited and skiing temporarily left my mind. Rosemary, Anita Mae and I talked nothing but dance-talk. Nobody concentrated on their classes. At 1:00, the day of the dance, our principal, Mr. Swithster, called the entire student body into the gymnasium.

"The teachers tell me you've been distracted from your work today," he said.

We snickered.

"Go home, kids," said Mr. Swithster. We looked around, unsure if we'd heard him correctly. "Go home and have a great time at the ball."

It was instant chaos as we flooded the gym floor, racing to our lockers to leave school early. It was the same time I left school every day.

Victor sulked and stomped into the house. He wasn't going to the ball. He had failed to meet Rosemary's deadline, and she'd found a new date, a boy from Old Lebanon named Bob Campbell. He was rumored to be the best jitterbugger around.

I had to admit, I felt a little bad for Victor. He just didn't realize who he was dealing with. If he was interested in Rosemary, he needed to up his ante, a lot.

I gave my mother her afternoon shot and snack, and she helped me put hot rollers in my hair. I wore them all afternoon while I prepared dinner. Steak and bread with baked potatoes. And apple crisp for Walter for dessert. Easy, quick and simple to clean. I needed to be ready at 6:30 sharp. Jeb wouldn't be late.

We sat at the table, ready to eat.

"When are you picking up Dolly and Patricia?" I asked Joe Jr., smirking.

Joseph and Abbott were going with the Andrews sisters.

"Six," they both said.

"Two sisters for two brothers. Did you plan that?"

Joseph looked at me warily. "No, but once Rosemary Heppe was off the list, I had to find someone else." Joe Jr. turned to Victor. "Ya know, Vic, you're an idiot not to ask her. Now she's going with an out-of-towner. What a waste."

"Eleven boys asked her to the dance," I said. "Rosie told me he's the best swinger around."

Victor's ears turned brighter crimson than ever before. Suddenly, he stood up, grabbed his chair and slammed it into the table. He left in a fury. Not wanting the night to be ruined, I turned the attention back to my oldest brothers.

"How did you decide who would take who? Pick a number out of a hat? Arm wrestle? Thumb war? Rock-paper-scissors?" I giggled, acting out rock-paper-scissors and ending with scissors.

"For your information," Joseph jumped up, grabbed me around the waist and tickled. "I'm taking Dolly."

"No!" I screamed with laughter, "Watch out for my hair!"

I washed the dishes with Walter. Ever since Walter saw me return from skiing, our understanding had deepened. I made him sweets, and his nods grew bigger. Pretty soon, somebody would ask what all the secret nodding was about. And, my father would tell me to use less sugar. So far, our chickens had cooperated by producing enough eggs to cover the extra cost.

Halfway through the dishes, my father entered the kitchen.

"Go take care of your mother, Vivian. Walter and I can finish here."

"Really?" I was astonished. Amazed.

"Really, get going! You have a big night ahead of you!" He smiled and lightly punched my arm.

I ran down the hall, brushing past my brothers. Abbott wore Joseph's old suit and Joseph wore my father's. It was a good thing Victor wasn't going. There weren't enough suits to go around.

"Now remember," I said to Joseph as I passed, "You're taking Dolly." He grabbed for my back, but I was too fast. I snuck into my mother's room.

"Vivian, honey, don't worry about me tonight. We can do this in the morning."

"No, Mother. Let's do this right." I disinfected her. I drew her night-time insulin shot and left it in the ice box.

"Are you sure Father will be able to give you your shot?" I was concerned.

"He does much more invasive things to the cattle, dear."

"I know, but he doesn't love the cattle."

My mother smiled, taking my hand. "He'll do just fine, dear. You'd better get dressed."

I ran to the basement and changed right there into my black satin gown with the delicate glass snowflakes. The satin clung to my body perfectly. I tore the rollers from my hair, and with my mother's help, put my waist-long locks into a fancy twist with tendrils that hung down my neck and shoulders.

I heard a knock at the door. It could only be Jeb. I looked at my mother.

"Well, don't just stand there. Go get him!" she said.

I ran to the door and opened it.

There, was Jebidiah Rettlan, freshly pressed and clean, shaved and fragranced. The boy whom I had played with and learned from since I was five. The boy who had taught me to ski jump in the dead of night. The boy whom with I had fallen in love.

"Hi, Vivian." His voice quavered just a bit. He was nervous!

I couldn't help but smile.

He stared at me, his eyes a big as a newborn calves. "Wow. I mean, jeepers, you're beautiful."

"Thank you, Mr. Rettlan." I curtsied. "And you, are quite handsome." I kissed his cheek, and his skin was the smoothest it had ever felt. He must have used his Christmas razor.

I took Jeb's hand. "Come on in. I'd like you to say hi to my mother."

26. READY TO GO

I pulled Jeb to my mother's room.

"Hi Walter," Jeb nodded as he passed my brother. Victor was nowhere to be found.

Mother had managed to sit up in bed and pull any stray hairs from her face. She looked okay. Not too sick.

"Hello, Mrs. Hostadt," Jeb said.

My mother took his hand. She covered it with her other hand. I held my breath.

"Hello, Jeb. It is good to see you. You look quite handsome. And doesn't Vivian look lovely?" My mother watched Jeb's response.

Jeb did one of his loud sighs. "Beautiful," he said. My father came into the room.

"Jeb, nice to see you." The two men shook hands. Walter peeked around my father's back.

"Mr. Hostadt, thank you for letting me take your daughter out tonight. I'll have Vivian home whenever you'd like." A curfew. I hadn't thought of that.

"How about midnight?" my father said. "Is that when the dance ends?"

"It goes from seven 'til twelve," I said.

My father thought for a moment, then reconsidered. "Okay then, how about 12:30. That way you won't miss a thing. Just make sure you let Joe Jr. know you're there. And if you leave before him, tell him so."

I hugged my father and gave my mother a tender kiss on her forehead. She placed her hand on my arm.

"Turn on your camera eyes, Vivian," she whispered. "I want to see everything."

We stopped in the kitchen while my father took our picture. Jeb helped me with my jacket. Taking his arm, we left the house. To my family's knowledge, this was the first time we'd ever gone out together, and especially, our first time out at night.

Of course, it wasn't.

It was, however, the first time we would be returning before 1:30am, without snow-pants, bruises or maple-carved skis.

27. THE SCHWARTZ BALLROOM

Jeb walked me to his father's car, kicking snow out of my way and guiding me carefully around ice. He opened my door, and I held his hand as I scooped up my dress and fell into my seat. I patted my hair and smoothed my satin as he walked to his door.

In the car, we couldn't help but smile.

"I like your suit," I said

"Thanks. It's my dad's."

Slowly, we made a wide circle through the driveway, oblivious to the faces watching us leave from the kitchen window.

"What do you think the Schwartz will be like?" I asked. I had never seen the inside of the ballroom.

"I don't know. I know they have a big chandelier. Is Victor going?"

"Nope. He didn't have the nerve to ask Rosemary, and then he was too mad to ask someone else when he found out she was going with Bob Campbell."

"That guy's supposed to be a swinger."

"Perfect for Rosie."

"I hope you'll still want to be my date after you see how he can dance."

I squeezed Jeb's hand. "Dancing is fun, but the question is, can he jump?"

Entering our small town, we immediately noticed a change in traffic. I had never seen so many cars. There were more black Model A's and T's than I could count, and some cars I'd never seen before.

"Wow, that's a new, 1938 Chevy Truck," said Jeb. "Look! There's a Gold Bug!"

This one I knew. Everyone in Hartford was well aware of the Kissel Kars. We slowly inched past the gold speedster.

"See the nickel trim? And the wire wheels? See the Kissel chrome yellow? They're known for that. Gold Bugs even have 'fat man' wheels."

"What?"

"Fat man wheels. The steering wheel can glide in or out so you can get in and out of your car easier. Did you know Jack Dempsey has one?"

"A fat man wheel?"

"No, a Gold Bug Speedster. And Ralph De Palma, the racecar driver. And Amelia Earhart had one, too."

I hadn't known Jeb was a car expert.

We found a place to park. Arm in arm, we walked to the Schwartz.

It was almost a round building, with a tower on top and windows encircling the entire complex. I tried to see inside, but the glass was either etched or covered with a thin drapery, so I couldn't make out any details. As we approached, I could hear the low, rumbling beat of drums. The ground shook below me.

"They've started!"

We walked through beautifully-carved doors bordered by stained glass, and I was taken aback by the brightness of the electrical lights that lit our entrance. The lights swooped out from the walls and twinkled and radiated their light into crystals that hung below them. The crystals had edges and points, and it didn't take more than a second for me to realize what they were...snowflakes.

They were perfectly sculpted, crystalline snowflakes. They beamed fireworks of white onto the walls, reminding me of glitter and glass beads, like the ones on my dress. They danced and lightly clinked to the growing beat of the drums.

No dead snow here.

I made mental notes for my mother. Jeb handed a man our tickets, and we checked our coats.

"Ready?" Jeb said as he held out his arm for me.

"I'm ready."

We walked to the doors leading into the ballroom and I gasped as the full, rich sound of drums, trumpets, saxophones and clarinets filled my ears with the most jubilant music on Earth.

We walked in, and Jeb and I both stopped at the perimeter of the dance floor and stared. Before us was a sight neither of us could have ever imagined growing up as dairy farmers in Southeastern Wisconsin.

People jumped and bustled, flying through the air as if they had wings, and I was blinded momentarily by the brightness of a 2,000 pound electrified chandelier hanging from the middle of a domed ceiling.

As if the snowflake lights in the entryway weren't enough, I burst into laughter as thousands upon thousands of glittering, ceiling snowflakes spun, twirled and swayed amidst currents of air cycling from spinning skirts and flapping dresses. It was a blizzard! A blizzard of twinkling white and silver dancing to the beat of the drums. This snow was the most alive it could be.

The tingy solo of a golden trumpet began. The musician blared his song through tightened cheeks as a light array of

drums and bass joined him. Four women appeared, aglow
in silver, fringed dresses. They swayed and slunk, swang
and sung, and I recognized the Cab Calloway famous,
"Minnie the Moocher's Wedding Day."

Here's some news that'll get you,
It's made to order for you.
I just bet it'll fit you,
Follow up these red hot blues.

Grab a taxi and go down,
Chinatown's on a spree;
Let me give you the lowdown,
This is really history.

Whenever folks in Chinatown start acting gay
There's something in the air that makes them feel that way.
Yeah, man, I heard somebody say
It's Minnie the Moocher's wedding day!

"Vivian!" I turned to greet a flashing red beauty.

"Hi, Rosie!" We wiggled with excitement.

"Isn't this fabulous? Don't you love my dress?" she
spun with her arms outstretched, very aware she took up
more room than three people.

Rosemary's dress screamed for attention: bright red and
low cut in the front with ruffled sleeves that draped just
slightly off her shoulders. It criss-crossed at her bosom and
fell alongside her body, every curve defined by a soft
clinginess. The line fell just below her knees in back, but
reached upward in the front, criss-crossing again and

climbing to her left mid-thigh. The hem-line was adorned with the same ruffles that caressed her shoulders, and they leapt and jumped with even the slightest movement. She showed more skin than any other girl at the ball. It was risqué.

A number of older woman frowned as they passed us. Rosie's dress was perhaps a little too revealing for Hartford.

"It's beautiful," I said. The band finished their song and began another with a deep saxophone lead. "Is Bob here?"

"Who?" said Rosemary, looking from person to person, carried away by her merriment.

"Bob!" I shouted.

"Oh, yeah. Hold on."

Rosemary ran to a punch bar. She returned just as fast dragging someone behind her. I was shocked to see Bob Campbell couldn't have been more than 13 years-old, skinny, awkward and smooth-cheeked.

"Vivian, Jeb, this is Bob Campbell." Rosemary looked her date up and down and rolled her eyes. We shook his hand.

"So, you're from out of town?" said Jeb.

"Old Lebanon," Bob squeaked.

This was the boy we'd all heard about? Maybe Rosemary had talked up her date a little. Or, maybe she hadn't known much about Bob before she agreed to be his date.

"Oh look!" shouted Rosemary. "There's Erv! Oh!" she gasped, "Mr. Skalstad is with him!" Rosemary pulled her dress down in the front. "Let's go." She yanked on Bob's jacket sleeve, but didn't wait for him.

"Rosie?" said Bob. He followed her general direction, losing her in the crowd. "Rosie?"

"I feel badly for that fellow," said Jeb.

"Don't feel too badly for him. He'll always be able to say he went to a dance with Rosemary Heppe. That's good for something around here, isn't it?" I said.

"To some people," said Jeb. "I'd rather just be with you."

And then he leaned down and kissed me. In front of everyone! It sent me spinning onto the dance floor.

"Let's dance!" I said.

I pulled Jeb onto the floor just in time for a new number. The beat bounced, pounding into my chest.

Jeb took my hands, and I was shocked to see he had some moves. He showed me how to "toe-heel, toe-heel" to the music.

"How do you know this?" I shouted.

"My sister showed me a few things."

We laughed, and he turned me into a spin that didn't work. Our arms twisted the wrong way and before I knew it, I was alone and facing the wrong direction. I turned to face Jeb, and he burst out laughing.

"My sister didn't show me that!" he said.

I felt more alive than ever. My shoulders shook. My arms flew. My legs moved faster and faster. I felt the firmness of Jeb's hold on my hand, or my shoulder or the small of my back.

"Let's go!" the band leader called. The music repeated, this time a tone higher.

Jeb grabbed my waist and took me close. Rosemary and Bob entered the floor, and Bob twirled Rosemary, spinning her in circles.

"One more!" the band leader shouted.

Jeb spun me around and around. Silvery snowflakes swirled above my head. I watched the chandelier move in circles until it appeared as one giant light above me. And then, with a fast bump thump, the music ended, and Jeb caught me in his arms.

The crowd erupted with electrified applause nearly as loud as the music.

"Let's get some punch!" called Jeb through the noise.

I followed him to the punch bar where Rosie was already pouring herself a cup. Bob was nowhere to be seen.

28. A BALL IN HIS HONOR

While chatting with Joe Jr. and Dolly, Mr. Maus interrupted us to formally open the dance. Dressed in a rented tuxedo, Mr. Maus's slicked back hair reminded me of how special the night truly was.

"I'd like to welcome each and every one of you to the most fantastic fund-raiser our community has ever seen! This ball is in honor of President Franklin Delano Roosevelt. It was he, who was brave and courageous enough to take charge of a country that had fallen. And it was he, who helped as many of us as he could along the way."

The crowd responded with applause.

"This ball is raising money to help a cause that is true and central to the President's heart, infantile paralysis. There is a black, wooden donation box on the edge of the stage. Any donations are appreciated. Ninety percent of the proceeds and monies raised at tonight's event will be donated to this cause. The other ten percent will go to renovating the east wing of the Schwartz Ballroom next summer."

"Everybody, hold onto your ginger ale. I'd like to introduce, Pep Babler and his Dance Orchestra!"

Mr. Maus handed the microphone to the leader of the band.

"Okay gentleladies and men, it's time to shake things loose and turn this ballroom into a fund-raising, dance celebration!"

Pep dropped his arms, and immediately, the piano man's fingers flew. The bass drums added their thunderous beat, and the crowd went wild. Men grabbed their partners by the hands and swirled them beneath Wisconsin's largest chandelier.

I felt Jeb's arm tighten around my waist, and he pulled me onto the dance floor. We found the beat and started our basic moves, not caring that we did the same steps and turns over and over.

Rosie and Bob ran up next to us. The small, mousie kid from Old Lebanon transformed into a Lindy-hopping showboat. Bob spun Rosie through his arms, around his back, through his legs and into contortions of moves that made my head spin.

Rosemary's red dress was on my right side, then on the left. She and Bob moved faster and faster, and I was pretty sure I saw the white lace of her bloomers as Bob tossed her into an aerial so high, her black and white oxfords pointed at the chandelier. The crowd danced crazily, but formed a wide circle around Rosemary and Bob, giving them plenty of room for their brilliance.

Jeb grabbed me at my waist. Lifting me up in the air, I squealed and laughed as I ended up over his shoulder. He spun himself around and around.

"What are you doing?" I yelled.

"Rosie and Bob's moves," he yelled back.

"Put me down!" I laughed and laughed. Back on the floor, I playfully pinched Jeb's cheek. "I never saw them do that move," I said.

"That one's too hard for them," Jeb smiled back.

Rosemary shook her red ruffles and clapped. Her shoes created a gray blur with points and twists that traveled the diameter of the circle while spinning and twirling in Bob's arms.

"Go, Rosie!" I shouted.

The number ended with deafening screams and stomping from the audience.

Rosie and Bob were the best dancers I'd ever seen.

"Bob," I said, "You're a great dancer!"

He smiled awkwardly. "Well, I…"

"Did you see my aerial?" interrupted Rosie. She leaned over to Bob. "A little more height would be nice."

I smiled uncomfortably at Bob, and so did Jeb. Rosemary didn't like her date at all.

"I hate having to lead all the time," Rosie complained. I couldn't believe her attitude. It was clear to me she was ruining her own night.

A couple walked past us, holding hands and leaning against one another.

"Don't get any ideas, Bob. You're not allowed to touch me except on the dance floor."

I held my breath. Bob looked longingly from Rosie to the punch bar, where a single, heavily-set girl stood alone.

"Rosie," said Bob, "You're a great dancer and all, but with how much you seem to dislike me, I'm sure you won't mind if I'm somebody else's partner tonight."

Bob walked away, straight for the punch bar. Rosemary looked at me, then Jeb, then back at Bob. We were shocked.

"Bob!" she yelled.

He turned around.

"You can't leave! You're my date!" Rosie put her hands on her hips and a pout across her face, expecting him to come back at once.

Bob shook his head.

"You weren't even my first choice!" she yelled.

Bob raised his arms, unconcerned. "You weren't my first choice either, Rosie."

29. SPECIAL DELIVERY

The orchestra didn't stop playing once, not even for an intermission. Jeb and I danced all evening. At first, Rosie had lots of boys asking her to dance. But by the end of the night, she spent most of her time alone at the punch bar, watching the others dance.

"I'm worried about Rosie," I said to Jeb, slowly dancing with him.

Jeb peered over toward the punch bar. Rosemary nervously looked side-to-side for anyone, anything to make her not alone.

"She'll be fine," he said. "And maybe she'll realize she brought her loneliness upon herself."

"Be nice, Jeb," I said. "It's not her fault she's the way she is."

"No?" Jeb smirked. "Then whose fault is it?"

But I didn't have time to answer him. At that moment, someone tapped Jeb on the shoulder.

"Excuse me, I'd like to have a dance with Vivian."

Jeb and I turned abruptly to see my father.

"Father!" I said. "Where? How? What are you doing here?"

My father laughed. "I had to make a special delivery. Don't worry, the boys are reading to your mother until I get home."

Jeb squeezed my hand and left me with my father.

"Jeb," I called after him, "Please dance with Rosemary." Jeb nodded.

My father gently took my hands and led me into the sweetest dance I could have imagined. I couldn't stop grinning. Resting my head upon his shoulder, I knew this was the best night of my life. Ever. I had Jeb, a dance with my Father and…the only thing that could have made it better, would have been my mother's presence.

When the song ended, my father walked me back to Jeb and Rosie, and I took Jeb's hands.

"Thank you, Father," I whispered into his ear.

"One of the best dances I've ever had," he said.

"Me, too."

I watched him leave, then came back to reality as the drums whipped into a final set. The night was almost over.

"Come on, Vivian," said my date, pulling me onto the dance floor.

I looked at Rosie, alone again.

"Are you okay?" I asked her.

"Yeah, oh yeah. I'm fine. You go ahead." She backed up, smiling thinly, looking tired.

I spun into Jeb's arms, looking back at Rosie to wave, but I only saw her back as she ran from the ballroom. Just as she reached the double doors, I finally understood what my father's special delivery had been. Rosemary ran straight into Victor.

"Victor!" Rosemary exclaimed. She quickly wiped a tear from her cheek.

"Uh, hi Rosie," Victor said. He anxiously tucked in his white shirt and straightened his tie.

"How did you get here?" Rosie asked, her lips trembling with humiliation from her botched night.

"My father dropped me off. Where's your date, Rosie?"

Rosemary couldn't hold in her tears any longer. She burst into a sobbing fit. "He left me for another woman!" she cried.

Victor looked around nervously, but the only ones watching were me and Jeb. He dabbed Rosemary's cheeks with his handkerchief.

"Rosie, I'm sorry I never asked you to the dance."

Rosemary looked up into my brother's eyes. "You were my first choice," she said softly.

"You were mine, too," he said.

And then he smiled. It was a sight I hadn't seen in almost a year. My grumpy, black-cloud brother smiled.

"Well lookie there," said Jeb. "Looks like Rosie and Vic might be each other's happy ending tonight."

Rosemary and Victor walked onto the dance floor. Taking her time to show Victor a few moves, the new pair unhurriedly began to dance, more interested in holding hands and being together.

With the last thump of the drum, my lips curved into a sleepy smile. I wrapped my arms around my date. My first dance had been perfectly wonderful.

Jeb found our coats while I hugged Rosie and said my good-byes to friends. I waved to Joseph, and Jeb and I made our way to his father's car. As soon as I hit the seat, I could have fallen asleep. Jeb laughed.

"Well, well, well. Dancing makes you even more tired than ski jumping."

"I can't move. I don't want to move." I took Jeb's hand. "Thank you, Jeb, for this night. I had so much fun."

He smiled at me. "Me, too. Now, let's get you home by your curfew so if I decide to ask you out again, your parents will say yes." I giggled.

He started the car, and I relished the soft rumble of the engine as compared to the loud music we'd heard all night long.

The kitchen light was a glowing greeting different from our secret outings. This time, my return was expected. We had to laugh when we saw Walter's head come into view, peeking outside.

"I think I like it better when we're together in secret," said Jeb.

"No watching eyes. And no rules."

The two of us walked to the front door.

"You're a pretty good dancer despite the fact you have two left feet," he said.

I laughed. "It makes it awfully hard for me to find a good pair of shoes."

"Can anyone see us here from the house?" said Jeb.

I giggled. "I don't think so. It must be killing them."

Jeb leaned down and kissed me, lightly, softly, as if a butterfly had landed upon my lips.

"I love you, Vivian," he whispered, his breath warm upon my face.

"I love you, too."

Jeb kissed me again and left.

I went into my mother's room and found she had eaten her entire night-time snack, and her shot had been administered.

"Vivian," she said, tired, but smiling. "You're back. How was the dance?"

I sat next to her and smoothed the wrinkles of her bleached sheets. "Absolutely, perfectly, wonderfully the best. Are you tired?"

"Not anymore," she said despite dark circles beneath her eyes. "I believe you owe me some memories." My mother shifted into a better position and closed her eyes. She was ready to listen.

From the beginning, I described everything. From when Jeb helped me with my jacket and my father took our picture, to Victor's heroic rescue. We sat for almost two hours, sharing and talking, holding hands and listening. And my superb recording skills didn't go un-noticed. Mother's eyes rewarded me with sparkles, laughter and love. She gasped when I acted out Rosie's conquest of the dance floor and even cried when I told her Jeb had told me he loved me for the first time.

I restocked the furnaces in my black satin dress and crawled into bed at 3:45am. I was thankful there was no school today.

In my bed, I thanked God for so many things. For dances and dresses, Jeb and music. For Rosemary and sequins, punch and drums. For ski jumps and snowflakes, love and most of all, my mother.

30. THE BIG ONE

With nine days before the annual ski tournament, jumping off the big one consumed me. If Victor could do it, I could do it, too. There was only one thing standing in my way.

Jeb.

Friday night, we jumped. I didn't push my luck at first, not wanting to make him angry. Rather, I worked it hard on the down-slope of the esker. From the top of the hill to the very bottom, I pushed it. I started with a running motion to build my speed, and I ended with a spray of snow that covered the straw bales. I was really getting good.

An hour later, I decided it was time to test my luck and run the jump past Jeb. We mounted the hill after climbing from a speedy trip down.

"What a great night for skiing. Almost a full moon. No clouds. Perfect visibility."

"Yeah, it's great," he said.

"Did you see my last descent?"

"You're getting pretty good, Vivian."

"I can't believe I can go so fast. Remember the first time on the practice hill?"

"How could I forget?" he laughed. "You've come a long way."

"And in a short period of time, too."

"That's true."

He wasn't catching on. I'd hoped he would offer the big one to me in celebration of how far I'd come, but he didn't.

"So, I'm feeling pretty confident on the esker now."

Silence.

"I think I could probably handle more of a challenge."

Silence.

"Even if it was in a series of baby steps."

Jeb couldn't hold it in any longer. He laughed. "Yes, Vivian. I think you're ready to start on the big one, BUT, only in tiny steps. Don't forget, you said you'd let me decide when and how far."

I ran to Jeb and squeezed him my hardest.

"Let's go!" I shouted.

We walked up five stairs of the jump. He stopped.

"We'll start here."

"But, we're hardly up at all."

"I know, but the take off is higher off the ground than the practice jump, and I want you to have a feel for the drop before we go up higher."

"But, I won't have any speed built up."

"I know. And you'll drop to the ground faster. That'll be good practice."

"For what?"

"Anything different than the practice jump. I'm telling you, these two jumps can't even be compared."

"But I like speed."

"Exactly."

I frowned. Mr. Rettlan wouldn't budge.

I took off my pout and replaced it with a smile. If guilt didn't work, I'd just have to inspire him to change his mind with my outstanding talent.

Jeb propped a ski on the jump so I'd have something from which to brace myself. I stood five feet up from the final angle of the slope and crouched low to the ground.

"Ready?" Jeb asked.

"Ready."

He took away the ski. The slope was steeper than I'd expected, because as soon as the ski was gone, I was moving.

Jeb was right. The angle at which the descent met the take off was sharper, and I was surprised by the different forces that pulled on my body. I flew for only a short time before landing hard, approximately ten feet down the esker. Still, I was going fast. I made it to the bottom and stopped with a flurry. I had done it! My first jump from the big one!

Jeb jumped down after me, and we walked up the esker together.

"You were right," I said. "The angle was different, and landing on the slope of the esker threw me for a second, too. You're a really good coach."

"Thanks." He took my skis. I caught his smile and we kissed right there.

We jumped Saturday night, too. I started at five feet up the slope, but progressed up to ten, then fifteen. I wanted to try twenty, but the slope at this height was too steep and difficult to start from.

By the next week, I was handling the big one with simplicity, at least from fifteen feet up the slope. Wednesday night came, and it was three days before the tournament.

"I think I'm ready to start at the top," I said.

Jeb looked at the top of the jump. It was super high. "I don't think so."

"Why? This is so easy. Starting at the top can't be that much different."

"It's too dangerous. Not yet, Vivian."

"But you saw me. I just handled the jump like it was nothing. I know I can do it."

Jeb did a noisy sigh. "No."

"But…"

"Vivian." He sounded angry now. "You may be ready, but I'm not. It's not just you here, you know." His response took me by surprise.

He needed more time to get comfortable with it. I knew I could do it. I knew I was ready. He probably did, too. But, his heart wasn't ready.

"Okay," I said. "Let's just stick with what we're doing for a while." I gave Jeb a hug and at first, he didn't really hug me back.

"I'm just worried about you," he said, tightening his arms.

"I know. But you know what I think? I think that maybe you're just afraid I'll jump farther than you. I think you're scared of me." I held my breath.

Jeb sniffed. "You couldn't jump farther than me if you had wings."

Jeb was back.

"Oh really? We'll see about that."

"But not tonight."

"Right. I'll just have to beat you on a different night."

"Fine. I'll bring my parent's camera."

Thursday night, we didn't jump. Friday came, and I found a note under my rock. I was so happy! I was itching to jump like a child with poison ivy.

I read Jeb's note:

Hey Vivian,

I hope you're not too disappointed, but I'm going to get some sleep tonight. I want to do well at the tournament tomorrow, and I'm nervous, too. I don't know why I am, because this year I've practiced more than ever.

I know you'll understand. You're amazing. Have I ever told you that before?

~Jeb

I just stood there holding my note and staring at the letters that suddenly didn't form words. Jeb didn't want to jump with me tonight. He wanted sleep.

Suddenly, I was awash with guilt.

"Of course he wants to sleep," I muttered. "How can you be so selfish?" He was competing tomorrow against some of the best jumpers in the state. In the nation!

My night crawled by at an agonizing pace. Dinner was boring, and I served my boys pot roast with potatoes, carrots and onions and raspberry-jam muffins. I disinfected my mother and felt like it took forever to cover every square inch of her body with sunshine water. And then to rinse, too. My skin crawled with aggravation as I tidied the kitchen and finished scrubbing the pot roast pan from its blackened deposits. Finally, it was ten o'clock, and I gave my mother her remaining shot.

I thought she was asleep, and I was glad because I hadn't really spoken much to her all night. My frustration was too distracting. I covered her with blankets and the woolen afghan from Aunt Betty. I was about to leave when she grabbed my hand.

"Vivian," she whispered, "Promise me when I'm gone, you'll look after Walter."

I froze.

"When you're gone?" I said.

"I won't be here forever." Her breathing was shallow and pronounced. I hadn't noticed the change in her state of health during her cleaning. I had been too consumed with my own life.

I stared at her face. Her eyes were closed and her head was especially far back against her pillow. It awkwardly pulled her mouth open, and her nostrils flared with each forced breath. I felt faint. I had to talk fast, get past this moment.

"I already do watch out for Walter, Mother. I give him special attention. And I make him sweets."

My mother's eyes opened, and her dry lips turned upward. "He always did have a sweet-tooth."

"Do you need some water?" I asked. I stood up, but she didn't let go of my hand.

"Just sit with me."

We sat.

Before my mother fell asleep, she said just one thing more. "You know Vivian, I love you more than a perfectly-sculpted snowflake. Beautiful and bright, sparkling and light. You are my snow."

I tried, but I couldn't think of anything to compare my love for her to.

Nothing was important enough.

Special enough.

"I love you, too, Mother," I replied.

We didn't say anything else. I just sat there, held her hand and watched her breathe. Her chest rose and fell, and I found myself so grateful that at that moment, I was with her while she was alive.

I sat with her until she slept. I made sure she kept breathing. Finally, at 11:30, I crawled into bed and lay there wide awake. My mind raced. My body prickled. I couldn't stop thinking about my mother's words.

They replayed over and over in my mind. "Beautiful and bright, sparkling and light. You are my snow."

Why hadn't I said anything back to her? I was nauseous with guilt.

Midnight came and went, and I couldn't lie in my bed a second longer.

My heart screamed.

I needed to get out.

I needed to jump.

31. GIRLS JUMP ALONE

I walked quickly in the night. A perfectly round, brilliant full moon filled the sky like an electrical light. It felt strange to be without Jeb, yet I was comfortable by myself.

I got to the big jump and didn't take any practice runs down the esker. Rather, I climbed fifteen feet up the slope and stared down the jump's decline into the darkened tunnel of trees where I would land. My body felt a little better, knowing I had already given in to the craving. The addiction would be satisfied.

I put on my skis and found it to be extremely difficult to position myself on the ramp without Jeb's help. I did, though, and as soon as I turned my skis to partner with gravity, I flew like an eagle.

Down the slope, off the ramp, I filled my tightened lungs with the freshness of wilderness air. I left my despair behind on streams of swirling snow, softly surrendering, drifting back to the ground. I was free.

I landed and laughed. I coasted down the hill and stopped at the straw bales.

"Girls do jump, Victor," I said out loud. "Girls jump alone."

I walked up the esker and didn't stop to rest before climbing the steps of the jump. I had not consciously decided I would jump from the top, but subconsciously I guess I had. I passed the midway mark and quickly found myself 50 feet in the air, perched like that eagle on a cliff in its nest. The jump slightly swayed back and forth, and goose bumps zipped up my spine. I attached my skis and overlooked my goal, my ski tips hanging over the edge of the cliff, my wings ready for flight.

I closed my eyes.

"This is it, Vivian," I said to myself. "This is the moment you've been waiting for." The big jump was mine, and it was perfect that I was doing it by myself.

I thought of Jeb. He would never have to know.

I thought of my mother. She was back at home, struggling to breathe in her tiny, diseased body. Just thinking about her, I struggled to breathe, too.

I thought of Victor. He was terrible to me. To everyone. His anger! It was horrific, and I hated him at that moment.

I hated life.

I hated death, too.

I bitterly stomped my skis against the snow and readied myself for my first complete jump from the big one. My anger would drive me and my weeks of practice would carry me.

I leaned forward, and even if I had wanted to change my mind, I couldn't have. I rattled down the jump at incredible speed, my body pushing downward, feeling as if it would be crushed into the ramp. I reached the take off and I allowed myself to coast off, suddenly feeling light and released from the shackles binding me to my life.

It was only a few seconds, that time I spent in the air, but it was the longest time I'd ever been airborne. I shouted as I flew, falling toward the earth, landing on the snow. I sailed down the esker and came to an especially abrupt stop, careening into the straw bales and landing on my back, staring at the moon.

I screamed with exhilaration. I cried, and I laughed. I kicked my legs. I had done it!

I had jumped off the big one.

And not from fifteen feet up, either. I had jumped from the top. I had flown! Like a bird or a butterfly or a plane. The feeling of flying had saturated me. I said a silent prayer for Amelia Earhart and her dead dreams.

I laid there for half an hour, staring at the moon, oblivious of the steady stream of silent tears that streamed down my cheeks and melted the snow beneath me. A small smile settled on my face and it felt natural, as if it had finally been invited to an exclusive party.

I was at peace.

I went home, stoked the fires and checked on my mother. She was sleeping, and I kissed her warm forehead. I had something now, something to compare my love for her to. I pressed my cheek against hers.

I whispered, "I love you more free than flying."

32. USE MY SLED

I awoke Saturday morning to what usually was my day
of chores. But, not this week. My parents were well aware
of the ski jumping competition, and until the last jump was
complete, we were all exempt from work on the farm that
could wait. Everyone got an early start on their jobs that
had to be done. The cows were milked. The pigs were fed.
I made everyone breakfast and took care of my mother.

It was an amazingly special day, and my father gave us
each enough money to cover the admittance fee: fifty cents.

"Are you coming to watch?" Victor asked as my father
handed out quarters.

"Yes, son. As long as your mother is feeling
comfortable, I'll be there." It was the first time I saw Victor
smile since the dance.

I spent extra time evaluating my mother. After the
previous night, and her statement about Walter, I needed to
know she was okay before I could justify leaving. She
seemed better. Her skin was pinker. Her breathing, easier.

"How are you feeling today, Mother?" I asked as I gave
her eggs and toast.

"Quiet. Light." I thought these were very strange words
to describe how she was feeling, but they were nice words.
Positive words.

"But, do you feel better? Stronger?"

"I feel calm."

Calm.

"Okay," I said. "Are you in pain today?"

"No dear, no pain. Just peaceful."

"Do you think you are well enough for me to go to the
ski tournament?"

Mother turned her head and smiled at me. "Yes, dear." It was a small smile. Soft. Real. "Just remember to take your camera. I want pictures when you get home."

"Yes, Mother," I said.

At ten o'clock, I gave my mother her shot and couldn't help but notice the relaxed look of her face as she napped. Her skin wasn't tight like sometimes, and she appeared to be very comfortable. I drew her shade over the bright, lively snow and scared a cardinal from her windowsill. Her room grew dark. I closed her door.

I had four hours.

I whipped on my outerwear and passed my father as I left the house.

"How is your mother, Vivian?" he asked.

"She looks good today. She's napping now. I administered her insulin, and she ate her snack. She should be good until 2:00."

"Do you think I can leave to see Victor jump?"

I understood his concern. "I think so. Just peek in on her and make sure she doesn't need anything."

"Okay. Bye sweetie. Have fun," he said.

"Bye, Father."

I left the farm behind me, traveling the familiar path to the esker. I played with the two quarters in my pocket, their coolness and smoothness reminding me of how special the day was. This was tournament day.

I was amazed at the number of people on the path. Cars lined our road north and south. Some had even pulled into fields. How would they ever get out?

The hill was packed with people, and I searched for Jeb, but couldn't find him. I paid my fee and found a chart at

Mr. Heppe's announcement stand. It listed the names of the participants and when each was scheduled to jump.

Jumps started at 11:00 with the Class A division, the adults. Class C started at 1:00, in which Victor's name was placed fifth behind Erwin's, Elmo Halverson's and two others.

Elmo was Erwin's only real threat. He was from Racine and had a reputation for flying. I was struck with disappointment when I realized that the Class B division didn't start until 3:00. I would be back home by then and wouldn't be able to see Jeb compete.

I felt a tap on my shoulder and turned to find Rosemary, afloat with cheer and radiantly smiling with Victor behind her. He looked away from me, as if willingly coming to talk to me was painful for him.

"Hi, Vivian!" Rosie grabbed me and hugged me with energy.

"Hey, Rosie. Victor."

"Vivian, Victor and I are looking for Elmo Halverson, the boy from Racine who's trying to beat Erv. Have you seen him?"

I shook my head. "No, Rosie. I wouldn't know him if I saw him."

"We just have to know what Erv's up against." Rosemary turned to Victor. "And you too, honey."

Honey? I raised my eyebrows and caught the slightest glance from Victor as he grimaced.

"Have you seen Jeb?" I asked, looking around.

"Rosie," said Victor, "I have to start practicing."

"Yes, dear, but I sure am thirsty for some hot chocolate." Rosemary pulled Victor toward the concession stand.

I just had to laugh.

I milled and chatted, but never saw Jeb. Finally, with 11:00 approaching, I secured a good spot by the esker to watch the Class A men compete. Each jumper was to jump three times, their flight distance measured and recorded. After the third jump, the participant in that division with the most flight distance was the champion, and won a new pair of skis. I knew my brother wanted those skis perhaps more desperately than I wanted his, and I hoped for his sake, he would find himself a miracle.

At 11:00, Mr. Heppe welcomed the crowd.

"Welcome, Ladies and Gentlemen, to the 1938 annual Hartford Ski Club Ski Jumping Tournament! It's a perfect day for jumping, and the men are ready to give you thrills and chills of daredevil feats. Before we begin, let's welcome Mr. Harold Skalstad, president of the Hartford Ski Club, and his fellow members as they bless the jump and open the competition."

Mr. Skalstad stood on the esker below the take off of the jump, and the other members of the Hartford Ski Club joined him. It was my first chance to see Jeb, and he stood with his arms over the shoulders of Victor and Erv. My heart skipped.

As loudly as they could, they broke into song, singing Mr. Skalstad's Norski ski song, "Yumpin' Yiminee."

Underneath the take off
One early Sunday morn
Stand a bunch of husky skiers
Who will yump and show their form

Oh, big and small, small and big
Watch them yump and hear them sing
Yah yah me saw naw
Yumpin' Yiminee!

Lutefisk and lefse, lutefisk and lefse
Yah yah me saw naw
Lutefisk and lefse

Yumpin' Yiminee!

We all chuckled, and the crowd murmured their approval for the green, ski-patched bunch.

It was time to start.

"The first jumper of the Class A competition will be, Harold Skalstad." The crowd applauded as he climbed the jump's steps and reached the top.

It was like clockwork, but still impressed me just as much as I watched his perfectly aligned body fly by.

"Look at that supreme form, folks," said Mr. Heppe.

I could do that! I shook my head with amazement, imagining myself jump off the big one by the light of a full moon.

Someone grabbed my elbow. Jeb.

"Did you see Mr. Skalstad's jump?" I gushed.

"He's a professional," said Jeb.

"He's amazing."

"Don't tell me you're turning in to a Rosemary Heppe," Jeb whispered.

I hugged Jeb from the side. "Don't worry. I just wish I could jump like him. I don't wish I could marry him."

The Class A men jumped for almost two hours.

"And the winner of the 1938 Class A division Hartford ski jumping tournament is, Charles Halter of Eau Claire, winning with a total of 241 points and having the most unbelievable jump of the day, measuring at 84.5 feet."

The crowd cheered its approval.

At 12:55, Class C started. My brother, Erwin, Elmo Halverson and thirteen others lined up to fly.

"Think Erv will win?" I asked Jeb.

"Yep. He's got it in the bag. Old Elmo's good, but not as good as Erv."

The competition started, and Erv jumped 60 feet. Elmo jumped 59. When it was Victor's turn, I crossed my fingers for him. He tore down the slope and coasted off the take off.

I shook my head. "It's short," I said.

Mr. Heppe kept us informed. "Okay, folks, it's the end of the first round, and Erwin Skalstad has the lead, but not by much. His current score is 60. Elmo Halverson of Racine is in second with 59. Harvey Bosby of Oconomowoc is in third at 57, and Victor Hostadt of Hartford is in fourth with 56.5 feet. It's still anybody's contest."

I felt helpless watching my brother lose his new skis. I grabbed Jeb's jacket sleeve.

"What, Vivian?"

"Victor doesn't have a chance unless he pushes off. He won't listen to me. Will you go tell him?"

Jeb smiled. "Let me get this straight. You want me to go tell your ornary, grumpy brother to push off?"

"Yes, please."

"Gladly." Jeb left for the top of the esker.

Erv was first. He stood at the top of the jump and the crowd silenced. He started his descent, and I held my breath, hoping to hear a glorious number like, "65 feet!"

He stumbled at the take off and launched into the air off balance. His arms out, his legs spread, he did everything he could to prevent himself from landing on body parts other than his legs. It didn't work. Erwin came down with his chest too far forward. He crashed down the slope.

Women screamed! Erv's body bounced and slammed and finally came to rest halfway down the hill. Erwin's father was the first to arrive at his side.

"Let us take a moment of silence to pray, folks," said Mr. Heppe.

We waited. We prayed.

Please God, please let Erv be okay.

I couldn't see if Erv was moving as there was a crowd around him, including Dr. Winston. I knew that if anyone could help Erv, it was him. He was a healer.

Ten minutes later, Mr. Skalstad and Mr. Rolefson picked Erv up in a sitting position, his legs dangling downward without his skis. Erv bravely waved to the crowd, even smiling, and I was so relieved. I guess no one knew the extent of his injuries, but at least he hadn't been too badly hurt. We clapped and cheered for him. But, his day of competing was over.

"There's no way you're jumping," said a woman behind me. I turned and looked at her. Her son, no more than nine, stood beside her.

"But Mother, I wouldn't crash," said her son.

"If Erv Skalstad, son of Harold Skalstad can crash, you'd never make it."

Suddenly, the jump had new meaning for me. Even Erwin Skalstad could have a bad jump. It was dangerous! And I had done it last night, alone. I was so stupid! What if I had fallen like Erv? No one would have ever known I needed help.

Five minutes later, the boys started again. Elmo jumped first.

"61 feet!" shouted the recorder. It was the longest jump for Class C so far.

It was Victor's turn.

He took his time, concentrating and focusing on his skis. Too long.

"He's chickening out," said the boy behind me.

I couldn't stop myself. I turned to face him. "He is not chickening out. He's concentrating. Maybe if you'd jumped before, you'd know these things."

"For goodness sakes," said the mother. She grabbed his arm and left.

"Come on, Victor," I whispered.

He leaned forward, and swooped down the jump. As he reached the bottom of the jump, I held my breath, and he pushed off with his legs for the first time ever. He had listened to me! Or, he had listened to Jeb. Regardless, he flew farther than he ever had.

The recorder shouted, "60 feet!"

I cheered! I watched Victor reach the bottom of the esker, and he slammed into the straw bales, Victor-style. The men in the crowd snickered, and we all watched him, his leg sticking up in the air and the other out of view.

We didn't laugh long, however, as it became quickly clear that Victor was in a predicament. His ski had caught the twine of the straw bale as he flipped over, wrenching his ankle and preventing him from getting up on his own.

Not as scared as I had been for Erv, I ran down the hill and found my father, helping Victor to a stand. The crowd cheered, and Victor limped to the side of the runway.

"I can't walk," he said, reaching for my father's shoulder. "I twisted my ankle."

Jeb ran up to us. "Do you think you broke it?" he said.

"I don't know."

My brother sank into the snow and did something I never would have expected.

He cried.

I thought I would shrivel into a rotten piece of meat. I was dying inside, watching Victor cry.

And then it hit me. His anger. His hatred. His obsession with skiing. Victor was exactly like me. He used skiing as his escape, and his grief had been expressed through anger. Of everyone in my family, Victor was having the hardest time accepting my mother's illness. I felt like a rat. Of all people, I should have been able to understand Victor's feelings. But I had missed them completely.

"I have to walk," said Victor, stopping his tears and forcing himself up.

"I don't think that's a good idea," said my father. "You should sit."

"No, I have one more jump. I have to jump."

Jeb looked at me with concern, and I could feel my eyes as round as last night's moon. I shrugged my shoulders to Jeb, as if to say, "I don't know what to do."

"Look," said Victor, "I'm jumping. I don't care if I have to jump on one leg. I'm jumping, and no one's going to tell me no."

Jeb and I offered our shoulders to Victor and slowly, we made our way up the esker. My father stayed behind at the bottom. Jeb tried to convince Victor not to jump, but Victor was insanely driven.

At the top, nine boys now gathered for the last round. Five others had dropped out. We sat with Victor behind a large evergreen, and he tried out his ankle.

"Argh." He groaned and jerked his leg upward, taking the pressure from his foot. "Ow!" he cried as his foot dangled without support. "I can't even let it hang. God, that hurts!"

Silence.

Victor sat and stretched his leg out in front of him. Silently, Walter joined us, peeking around a tree. No one knew what to say.

"Dammit. God dammit!" Victor pounded the snow and couldn't help but shriek as the motion wiggled his foot. "I can't jump," he surrendered. He cried again. Walter looked at me with fear.

"What if I change the order of the jump and ask Mr. Heppe to announce you last? Will that give you enough time?" said Jeb.

Victor shook his head and wiped his eyes. "I don't need a different spot. I need a different ankle!" Victor wiped his nose and hung his head in shame. He knew he had a chance to win, with only he and Elmo still vying for the championship.

I thought about his comment. A new ankle. And then it hit me. I knew what we had to do. I knew what I had to do.

I ran to Jeb and whispered into his ear.

"No," he said.

"Why not?"

"Because that's the craziest idea I have ever heard, Vivian."

I wasn't ready to back down. We had to get moving if my plan was going to work. I ran to Victor and knelt beside him. I placed my hand on his shoulder and he looked into my eyes with utter sorrow. I had to do it.

"What if I jump in your place?" I said.

"What?" he said.

"No, Vivian!" Jeb was angry now.

"You can jump?" said Victor.

I nodded. "Yeah."

"When?"

"At night."

"With my skis?"

"Yes."

Walter's mouth dropped open. I stared at Victor, his eyes narrowing and his mouth tight.

"Can you do it? Jump off the big one?" he said.

"Yes," I said.

"No, you can't!" Jeb was on his feet now. "You've never even jumped further than a quarter of the way up! It's too dangerous."

"Yes, I have."

"What?" said Jeb. The anger on his face frightened me. I had never planned on telling him.

"Last night. I came here and jumped from the top. I did it, Jeb! I did it, and I can do it again!"

"By yourself? You jumped by yourself? Are you trying to get yourself killed?"

Walter took a few steps back from the conflict. His face, as white as the surrounding snow.

"Look, I know I shouldn't have done it. But, I did. And, I jumped far! I want to do this. I'll wear Victor's jacket and hat, and no one will ever know it's me. We look exactly the same!" Victor and I had the same Sicilian face. People had thought we were twins! "I can pull it off, Jeb! I know it!" I pleaded with Jeb, looking at Victor for support, but he was too shocked to give me any.

"This is crazy," said Jeb. "You have lost your mind. Even if you did jump, what would you do at the bottom when people approached you? Turn into a boy? You can't hide who you are up close."

This was true. I would be discovered, and then we would certainly be disqualified.

Silence.

I didn't have a response for Jeb this time. It looked as though he had won. I wouldn't jump.

"I'll be at the bottom," said Victor. "Behind the straw bales. Hiding. When you get there, come over the top, and we'll switch jackets. I'll stand up like I did the jump."

I smiled with hope and looked at Jeb with a desperation and need unlike any other. "Please Jeb, please help me do this."

"You'll have to limp up the stairs," said Victor, still plotting, "if anyone's going to believe it's me."

I nodded and searched Jeb's face for approval.

Mr. Heppe made an announcement. "And now, the final round of the Class C competition. First to jump is, Elmo Halverson."

"There's not enough time," said Jeb, reading my mind. "Victor can't get to the bottom before you'd jump. He can't even walk."

I looked at Victor. He shook his head, accepting defeat. I felt my tears coming back again.

Walter came forward, from around his evergreen. "Use my sled."

The decision was made.

Victor tore off his jacket, and I threw him mine. I braided my hair and tucked it into Victor's jacket. I grabbed his skis and hid behind the tree. I would stay there until Victor's name was announced so the other boys wouldn't talk to me.

"55 feet!" the recorder shouted.

"Elmo jumped short!" I said, startled. He'd played it safe. Maybe Erv's crash had scared him.

I flashed a look at Victor and Jeb. "What do I need?" I said desperately.

They thought for a second. "58.5 to tie," said Jeb. "59 to win." He shook his head. "You can't do it, Vivian. That's a long jump, even for a boy."

"Look, I can jump. Now, go!"

Mr. Heppe announced, "Jumping second for Class C is, Harvey Bosby."

"Go!" I shouted.

"You'll have to push off!" Victor yelled.

I sniffed. I didn't need to be told to push off.

Victor bit his lip in pain as he slid onto Walter's sled. Jeb and Walter took off running, pulling my brother behind them as he tried to support his ankle. As they disappeared from sight, Victor moaned.

It didn't seem like more than a minute before the recorder shouted, "54 feet!" The crowd applauded, and I waited breathlessly for my turn.

I checked my jacket and hat and pushed any loose hairs under the wool. My snow pants were the same as Victor's, so they didn't matter. My boots were brown, while Victor's were black. But, they were mostly covered by my snow pants, and would be disguised with skis.

"Hopefully no one will notice," I reassured myself.

"Jumping third for Class C is, Victor Hostadt."

I closed my eyes, clutching the familiar skis to my chest.

I walked out from behind the evergreen with a pronounced limp to my right leg. The other boys were searching for me, and I nodded to them as I hurriedly hobbled past. I got to the steps and began the climb, limping the whole way, and aware down to my goosebumps, of the silenced crowd behind me. They were watching and waiting to see if I could do it. That is, to see if Victor could do it.

I got to the top and slowly strapped my skis to my boots. I prepared myself, trying to ignore the sea of faces watching me. I felt sick.

Suddenly, I saw something very bad. Jeb, Walter and Victor were not to the bottom of the hill yet. I could see Jeb running, pulling the sled behind him, but the boys had gone widely around the crowd and wouldn't have enough time to get to the bottom. I had to stall.

I unstrapped my skis, and the crowd murmured. I walked a third of the way down the jump and pretended to smooth a lump of snow, just like I had seen Mr. Skalstad do weeks ago. I smoothed the flat surface even smoother. Suddenly, I noticed movement at the base of the steps. I turned. It was Harold Skalstad.

"Everything okay, Victor?" he called as he climbed the steps.

I lurched forward, almost forgetting to limp. "Yeah," I called in a deep voice. Why wasn't he with Erwin? I waved him off and started for the top again. Mr. Skalstad watched me for a minute, then left. I hoped it was enough time.

At the top, I strapped my skis to my boots and saw that Jeb, Walter and Victor were now at the bottom, but trapped behind a group of people near the straw bales, including my father.

"They can't get there," I said. I had to divert attention.

I reached my arms above my head and whooped with aggression. I pounded my fists into my chest and shook my arms while I growled and groaned, lifting my right ankle. I made a spectacle of myself, but I breathed a sigh of relief

as I saw that my behavior worked. The entire crowd
observed me with intrigue, including my father. The three
boys slipped behind the straw bales. Only Jeb and Walter
emerged.

Victor was waiting.

I was ready.

I prayed to God for a safe landing and bent my knees.

"This is for you, Mother," I whispered.

Placing my arms behind me, I leapt forward to quickly
accelerate.

I plummeted down the slope and reached the bottom
with frightening speed. Without a moment to spare, I
pushed with all my strength and hurled myself into the air.
I felt a lift I'd never felt before, and I knew I was jumping
far. I wasn't used to extra airtime, though, and I bobbled
and fought to maintain my balance. I plunged downward,
approaching the esker in a flash of reflected light.

My skis found snow, and I dashed down the runway,
heading straight for the straw bales. I tried to slow myself,
but it didn't work. I was going too fast!

I didn't have to fake my collision. I hurtled into the
straw bales with a crash and pushed upward, launching my
body over the top.

I'm not sure exactly what happened next. I hit the
ground and couldn't see for a moment. Everything went
black. I also couldn't breathe. I felt Victor's hands on me.
He ripped the jacket from my body and pulled my hair as
he grabbed his hat.

He jumped up and screamed, "Yeah!" The crowd
erupted into a frenzy of cheers and calls, whistles and
applause.

Victor came back down to me, and I could just barely make out his blurred face. "Get the skis off!" he said frantically.

Victor detached the skis, and Jeb must have held the crowd at bay because as soon as the skis were free, Victor grabbed them and darted out of the landing area. He limped and bared his teeth with pain, on fire with life.

"59 feet!" the recorder shouted. The crowd cheered again, and Victor hollered with triumph.

He had won.

33. LATE AGAIN

"Jumping fourth for Class C is, Jon Nelson."

I heard someone approaching.

"Vivian, are you okay?" It was Jeb. "You have to get out of there."

I nodded and felt myself coming to. Jeb stood and pretended to restack the straw bales for the next skier.

"Okay," he said, "Now." We walked out together, as if I had been there with him the whole time. Nobody noticed.

We walked to the side. Walter was there, too.

"Are you okay, Vivi?" said Walter's white face.

"I did it," I said.

I leaned over and put my hands on my knees to stop swaying. I stepped side to side, still feeling uncertain of my balance. "It wasn't pretty, but I did it."

Silence.

Then Jeb laughed. I squeezed my eyes, trying to make them focus. Walter laughed. I must have looked pathetic, because they laughed until their insides hurt.

"Vivian Hostadt, have I ever told you that you amaze me?" Jeb said. He kissed my head and held my hands. Walter's color returned.

"I think you've said that once or twice before," I smiled.

"Okay, have I ever told you that I think you're crazy?"

"I think just once." I laughed too.

"Are you sure you're okay?"

"Yes," I assured him. "I'm fine."

"I have to get ready to jump," he said. "Will you cheer for me?"

I knew Class B started at three o'clock. I gasped and pulled up my jacket sleeve. I peered to see the time on my ladies wristwatch. 2:30pm. I was late for my mother.

"I'm late!"

I ran. Dizziness and all.

"Vivian!" Jeb called after me. "Do you want me to come?"

"No!" I kept running. "Good luck!"

I ran the whole way.

34. DEAD SNOW

I had never run a mile before in my life.

My lungs singed with fire. I sprinted to the farmhouse, my heart desperate because I was so so late. I ripped open the door and didn't bother to take off my outerwear. I went straight to the kitchen and retrieved my mother's insulin from the ice box. Grabbing her pre-made sandwich, and without losing a second, I went to her room.

I opened the door and was surprised to see my mother's window shade still closed. It was dark, and she was napping. I quickly noted she hadn't eaten her snack, which sat on her bed-side table. I pulled down her sheets and lifted her housecoat.

I pressed the plunger, and as I did, I noticed a bump beneath her skin. It took me a second, but it was the same location of the dose I had given this morning. I checked my mother's ledger to make sure. Yes, I had recorded it. It was the same spot.

I was confused. Sometimes there would be a bump where the medicine went in, but it always went down with time. This time, the bump had not gone down. The medicine was still there.

My mother's body hadn't used it.

"Mother?" I whispered.

I could hardly breathe. She looked so peaceful. Her skin was loose and her mouth, relaxed. She was in the exact same position as this morning.

"Mother?" I said again.

I turned her toward me, but was repelled by her cool skin. It was unnatural.

My mother was dead.

I sat down, dumbfounded, and stared at her hand. It was motionless. Those were the hands that knew everything. Those were the hands I depended on to teach me about life. And love. They were useless now. I was alone.

My mother was dead.

"Dear God," I cried, "please accept your newest angel of light, Birgetta Hostadt."

I screamed. I couldn't suppress my pain. I had no reason to. I placed my head upon my mother's bony chest and wept.

I raked the woolen afghan carefully covering her body. It had kept her warm during these last weeks. It had kept her company. The blanket hadn't been late! But, I had. My crying was laden with guilt, and I wept with burdened helplessness.

My mother was dead.

"No!" I cried. "Don't go, Mother. I need you here! Stay with me!" I sobbed.

I wept until a calm sorrow overtook me. I needed to take care of my mother. I had to finish my job.

I drifted to the kitchen and removed my outerwear. Filling my bowl with hot water, I grabbed two clean towels from the bureau and went back to my mother's room. I added 30 drops of iodine and hypnotically watched as the drops curled heavily into the water. I soaked my towel in sunshine water and went to work. It would be the last time I would disinfect my mother. I wanted her to be fresh before anyone saw her.

I worked through newfound tears and rinsed her from head to toe.

"You would have loved the tournament, Mother," I said softly. "Victor won. Well, I won. I can ski jump, Mother. I can jump with the boys."

With great difficulty, I dressed her in clean pajamas. I washed and combed her hair. She was ready now. Ready for the world to see. Ready for the world to know.

I picked up our telephone.

"Dr. Winston's office, please," I said. Within moments, I was connected. And ironically, because of Erv's fall, Dr. Winston was there on a Saturday.

"Hello?" he said. "Dr. Winston's office."

"Hello, Dr. Winston. It's Vivian Hostadt."

"Hi, Vivian. Is everything okay?"

"No, Sir. I just got home and…" It was so hard. "My mother, she's gone." Saying those words crumpled me against the wall, and I fought not to cry on the phone.

"Are you sure?"

"Yes, Sir. I'm sure."

"I'm sorry, Vivian. Your mother was a wonderful person. I'll be there soon."

"Thank you."

"Good-bye."

I hung up the phone and fell to the floor, scraping the walls with my fingernails. I was so involved with my crying, I didn't hear the front door open.

It was my father.

His face slackened when he saw me. His arms dropped to his sides.

"She's gone," I sobbed. "I was late."

The rest of the afternoon was a blur. My father stayed in my mother's room until Dr. Winston arrived, talking quietly, wishing my mother a peaceful journey to heaven.

The boys trickled home one by one and learned the news. They joined my father, each taking their own turn saying good-bye. Surprisingly, almost everyone seemed peaceful. Scared, perhaps, like I saw in Walter's eyes. Sad, of course, like I saw in Abbott's eyes. But peaceful. Except for Victor. He looked hollow. Empty.

My mother had been in so much pain. For so long. They all were ready. I believed my mother had been ready, too.

"I feel calm," she had said. "Take care of Walter," she had said. She had known. She had waited until the house was empty, and she was by herself. She had died on her own terms. She had died peacefully.

I carried my cold sunshine water outside and poured it into a snowdrift of white. A newly falling snow littered my eyelashes, and I watched as the snow, bit by bit, covered the yellow antiseptic. Clouds thickened, and as the stained, yellow sunshine disappeared from my drift, my throat tightened.

The snow was dull and dreary. It just lay there, concealing the last evidence I had of my interactions with my mother. No shimmering flakes. No sparkling diamonds. Anger filled my soul, and I threw my bowl against the foundation of our house. It shattered.

Dead snow.

35. A FUNERAL

The funeral was on Tuesday, and I worked through my grief by cleaning everything in sight. I scrubbed, polished and swept. I scoured, bleached and washed. And then, I did it again. By Tuesday, the house was immaculate.

My father prepared the casket in the living room. He arranged candles around it to give more light, but my mother was still deeply in shadows.

"Vivian, don't we have anymore candles?" he shouted.

I scurried through cabinets and drawers. I found one candle stub left. I gave it to him, and he sniffed, then threw it against the wall. He stomped past me, slamming the front door behind him.

I watched him through the kitchen window as his legs stuck out from the inside of his Model A. He jumped out, cursing.

"Vivian!" he yelled.

I ran outside. "Yes?"

"Get me my screwdrivers."

I ran into the house, pulling the only screwdriver I knew of from a cabinet. I ran it outside, ignoring the wind that cut into my eyes.

"Thank you," said my father, taking it gently.

I went back into the house, watching his legs again until he finally emerged, carrying a small box. He stomped past me again, into the living room.

When I finally checked on him, my mother lay quietly beneath a sharp beam of light.

"What's that?" I asked.

"The dashboard light. I used the hot shot battery."

I stared at my mother, her ghostly face making me weak.

"Father," I said quietly, "would you get the box down from the attic for me?"

Sadly, my father nodded and retrieved the box for me. It was the second time I would wear my mother's black dress. I lowered the hem and removed the sparkling beads that seemed too joyful now. It was perfect for a funeral.

My father greeted visitors with acceptance. Although my mother's casket was in our living room, the fog of death that had plagued us for over a year was gone. I felt it, too. I sickened myself with guilt over my feelings. I should have been more upset. My mother deserved my grief. Perhaps we had been grieving already for a long time.

Visitors kept coming, and I did my best to talk with them. They were a somber bunch, all weighted down in their heavy black.

"Vivian, honey pie. How are you holding up?" said Aunt Betty. She squashed me into her round belly.

"The same," I said. "My spirits are high." I knew it was a strange response, but it was my automatic one, and paradoxically, seemed to fit. Grace stood by her side.

"I'm so sorry, Vivi," she said.

"I know," I said.

"If there's anything I can do, I will," she said. "I pray for her."

"Thanks, Gracie. I do, too."

Jeb's entire family came to pay their respects. It was awkward for me to see them at my mother's funeral, but his mother was especially nice and brought me a hand-embroidered handkerchief.

"Please come over for dinner sometime, Vivian," she said.

"That would be nice," I replied, but knew I couldn't. I
had to serve my boys their dinner.

Dr. Winston arrived, and he held my hands as he spoke
to me. "You did a brilliant job taking care of your mother,
Vivian. She lived as long as she could, and that was
because of you. You know it was time for her to go, don't
you?"

All I could do was nod.

"Her death was not your fault," he said. "You even kept
her from getting an infection. That in itself was a miracle.
Vivian, she would have died months ago if it hadn't been
for you. This wasn't your fault."

He squeezed my hands as he said, 'wasn't your fault.' I
heard him, but I didn't believe him. Of course it was my
fault.

I was late.

I continued nodding and shaking hands as the town of
Hartford courteously made their appearances. They
streamed into our living room to view the casket.

Victor sat in the corner of the living room. He didn't
shake anyone's hands, rather sat there, staring at Mother's
face as if she had cast a spell on him. I remembered him
crying at the tournament. I knew he was hurting. No
custom-made skis could take away his pain.

I felt badly for Victor. I no longer thought of him as
hating me. Or even angry. He was just plain sad. He'd
never handled Mother's sickness well. It looked like he
wouldn't handle her death well either.

Jeb stayed in the kitchen. The air tasted stale and I
smelled a pipe. I thought I might get sick as I struggled to
breathe. The somber heaviness was suffocating.

I stumbled toward the kitchen.

"Let's go outside," Jeb said.

The cold air knocked life back into me, and I held Jeb's arm. Hefty, gray clouds billowed toward the ground, shadowing everything in sight. I winced. More dead snow.

"I can't go back in there," I said.

"I know."

"Those people, they're frightening."

"I know."

"I can't stand that light on her face. It's so…" I buried my face into Jeb's jacket.

"I know."

But I did go back in. I shook hands until the last people left our home, and my father returned the dashboard light to his car. Jeb left.

We each took one more turn, my brothers and I, saying good-bye to my mother. I bent over her, placing her Christmas pillow in the casket.

"This is to keep you company," I whispered. "I love you sweeter than cinnamon applesauce and yellower than daffodils… toastier than a warm fire and brighter than autumn colors. I love you, Mother."

Together, with all of us helping, we closed her casket and carried it out to the barn where it would stay until spring.

36. ONE MORE STOP

"Vivian, where's my fishing pole?" called Walter.

I pointed to the red shed. I was thankful when the ground thawed and the snow disappeared. Crocuses, tulips and daffodils peeked from the earth, and I felt my first breath of new life. My mother's casket left our barn and found a new home at St. Olaf's cemetery. Mother was gone, but life went on.

I found more time on my hands than I knew what to do with. No more shots. No more disinfecting. No more heavy amounts of laundry. My routine, as hard as it had been, was gone. I felt lost for months until I found ways to fill the void. I spent much of it with Jeb and the rest of my time studying. Turns out, I was able to graduate in December of my senior year, six months early.

Rosemary and I embraced as I left Hartford High School for the last time.

"I told you that you studied too much," she said. "Now I have to get through the next six months without you."

"I'll miss you too, Rosie. Have you heard from Victor?"

Rosemary shook her head. Victor had enlisted in the Army the second he graduated from High School last year.

"Not since he was sent to Europe. Vivian, do you think he'll be okay?" Rosie's eyes filled with tears. The German Reich was invading everywhere.

I nodded. "Victor is strong, Rosie. And smart. He'll be okay."

Rosie nodded and gave me one more hug. I waved good-bye as I ran down the walkway to my father's car.

Even though Victor had received his coveted skis at the tournament the day my mother died, my jump had not salvaged our relationship. Jeb listened to my sorrow.

"But Vivian, you and Victor not being friends isn't because of you," he said.

"Maybe it is."

"Does he talk to your brothers?"

"No."

"Does he talk to your father?"

"Not really."

"See, it's not your fault."

And yet, I remembered how we used to play and hold affection for one another. Splashing at Turtle Lake. Searching for green and gold-spotted cocoons on milkweed plants. I still had hope we would be friends someday.

Jeb and I applied to colleges. The day arrived when we both held our letters from the University of Wisconsin-Madison. So far, he hadn't been drafted.

"You first," said Jeb.

"Okay." I opened one end, pulled out my letter and read silently. I looked at him with worry. "I'm accepted," I said. "You open yours."

Jeb opened his letter and pulled it out. He read silently, too, and looked at me as if it was the end of the world.

"What?" I said. "What does it say? Tell me!"

"I'm in."

I screamed and hugged him. Madison was our first choice, and we would start right away in the winter term.

January arrived, and I promised my family I would write and come home often. My father was proud of me, his first child to receive a college education.

Jeb and I packed lightly. Jeb threw my suitcase into his truck.

"Anything else?" he asked.

I looked around. "Just my bookshelf. It's on the porch."

Jeb returned with the bookshelf, a broad grin across his face. "Nice shelves," he said.

My bookshelf was smoothly carved from maple and had slightly turned-up ends. It had seen the earth from a bird's view. Now, it would hold my books and future, as its shelves had once been strapped to my boots and held my heart and past.

I kissed Walter's cheek and hugged him extra tightly. I would miss him the most. I knew he would miss me.

"I'll send you cookies," I said, looking up into his eyes, as he had grown.

"Remember my favorite?" he asked.

"Gingersnaps. And maybe you could come visit me on campus sometime."

"Sure, maybe. But I have a lot to do on the farm," he said.

I didn't really worry about him. Walter was growing up and didn't need me as much as he used to. He was milking cows with the older boys now, and this year, he would independently help with the new season's harvesting. He did manly work, now. Farmer's work. And Walter was proud to be a farmer.

Lastly, I hugged my father. He smelled of hay and the iodine he used to cleanse the cows before milking. A shot of pain coursed through me as it was also my mother's smell. My father was alone now, and suddenly, I didn't want to let him go. This was the man who had purchased an electric washer for me to make my life easier. This was the man that had shared a Wisconsin State Fair cream puff with a young woman named Birgetta years ago. This was the man that my mother loved with all her heart. I did too.

"I love you, Father," I said. "If you ever need me to come home and help with things, just let me know."

"We'll be fine, Vivian," he said. "Ms. Paulson is going to help with some of our dinnertime meals, and the boys will do some of the housework. They know they have to."

I didn't like his response. I'd already been replaced, before I was out the driveway. This was what I wanted, though. My freedom! Yet as my father spoke so nonchalantly of my departure, I felt the need to stay. I wouldn't, but I felt it.

"The latch on the stove is sticky. You have to press it in a little before you can open it."

"Okay. Don't worry." My father smiled, and I felt my eyes well with tears. I embraced him one more time.

"I love you, Father," I said again.

"I love you, too, Vivian." We hugged a long time, and as I finally lessened my embrace, my father pulled me close, his voice whispering into my ear. "Just so you know, I was there, too. I saw it. I know what you did."

I shuddered and held my breath.

"Nice jump, Vivi," he said.

I couldn't help but smile. My father laughed, a big guffaw, and smacked my shoulder a few times like I was one of the boys.

He knew! But how? Bewildered, I waved to my brothers and climbed into Jeb's truck.

As Jeb and I pulled from my father's driveway, I waved one last time and felt a heaviness lift from my shoulders. I was sad I was leaving my family, but happy I could finally have my own life.

"He knew," I said, shaking my head with disbelief. "He knew the whole time."

"Knew what? Who?" said Jeb.

"My father. He just said, 'Nice jump.'"

Jeb laughed, amused with my confusion and shock. "He's your father. Father's know things. Don't be so surprised."

I guess Jeb was right. My father had been there for the jump. Maybe he'd noticed my form had been different than Victor's. Maybe he'd been suspicious when "Victor" had been able to jump despite such a bad sprain.

"One more stop?" Jeb asked.

"One more stop," I said.

We drove to Hwy O and turned right, quickly coming upon St. Olaf's. The sun shone brightly, and I narrowed my eyes as headstones and their accompanying drifts of snow blinded me. We stopped.

"Would you mind staying in the car?" I asked.

"Sure, Vivian. Take your time."

I walked to my mother's gravesite and sat on a blanket. I read her inscription:

Birgetta Katarina Hostadt
Beloved Wife and Mother
September 28, 1902-February 2, 1938

I wiped the words and sat in silence, feeling my mother's presence. I wondered if she spent her days with God. I closed my eyes and imagined her before she became sick.

I remembered the stunning smell of freshly picked garden oregano my mother would add to her spaghetti sauce, or the smooth firmness of harvested tomatoes rolling in my hands. I had loved searching for watercress with her by the warmth of Turtle Lake, or puckering to a hot, sour, currant muffin. My senses spun designs and patterns with my memories.

A patchwork of clouds arrived, and I was stirred by the coolness of tiny snowflakes upon my cheeks. I watched them fall, so gently, so delicately. One rested upon my coat, and I studied it. It reminded me of my mother and her last comparison she had made of her love for me.

"I love you more than a perfectly sculpted snowflake. Beautiful and bright, sparkling and light. You are my snow," she had said.

"Hello, Mother," I said. I blew the snowflake from my coat. "I have news for you."

I looked back toward Jeb's truck, and he was still there, waiting for me.

"Do you remember, Mother, when I made you a promise? Well, I'm here to complete it. Jebidiah Rettlan and I are to be married, Mother. We are engaged."

I smiled and rubbed the gold band that encircled my finger. I talked to my mother more, explaining to her that I was going to college. I promised to talk to her every day.

"Don't worry, Mother," I said. "I'm not leaving you, I'm just leaving to find myself. You'll be with me every step of the way."

"I love you smoother than cream, stickier than honey and brighter than a full moon." I laughed. "I love you, Mother."

I picked up my blanket. I felt light. I was happy. I took a deep breath as I sprinkled sunflower seeds on my mother's headstone.

As I walked away, I kicked the snow. I smiled and spun as millions of pieces of silver immersed me within a dazzling assortment of tiny, perfectly sculpted, crystalline snowflakes. Billions of flakes, each bending and reflecting the sun's light into a sea of sparkling diamonds.

Jeb and I drove away into that snow.

Peace snow. Freedom snow. Life snow.

Have you ever walked in a newly fallen snow?

THE TRUTH ABOUT MY WOODEN WINGS

One cold day in February, I saw a picture lying on my parent's kitchen counter. I studied it. I was hooked like a fish or stuck like glue, you might say. The intrigue of this picture captured my full attention, and even before I knew anything about it, a story began to form.

This picture had been supplied by my parent's eighty year-old neighbor, Erwin Skalstad, and illustrated a sight that had not been seen in physical form for almost 60 years. The Hartford Ski Club ski jump.

Erected for the first time in 1930, the jump would be built, rebuilt and moved three times before finding its final resting spot. Overseeing the construction of the jump was Mr. Harold Skalstad, a Norwegian immigrant who arrived on Ellis Island off the boat, The Tietgen, on August 31, 1909 when he was nineteen years old. Soon enough, Mr. Skalstad found himself married and settled in Ashippun, Wisconsin, about eight miles southwest of Hartford.

Having grown up with ski jumping, Harold didn't waste any time. The jump was 50 feet high and rested on the top of a steep esker with a 125 foot runway. It was constructed of pine lumber and tamarack poles. Thick, sturdy wire connected the jump to surrounding trees and earth to keep it from tipping over. Traveling up the jump, alongside the ramp, were small boards nailed to the slope. These acted as makeshift "steps" for the skiers to climb to the top. At the top was a tiny platform on which to prepare to fly.

Jumpers from the Ashippun Ski Club, which later became the Hartford Ski Club, adorned green patches made of felt. The words, "Hartford Ski Club," encircled the green in white letters, and a skier of white felt rested in the center.

Harold's wife made these patches along with numbers to identify the skiers. The patches were attached to the backs of the skier's jackets with safety pins.

Harold Skalstad also oversaw the construction of maple-carved skis in the basement of a neighbor's house. Augers, planers, chisels and carving tools created perfectly balanced skis that the skiers could purchase for a small fee. These skis attached to one's boots with leather straps. They did not have quick-release bindings. If one fell, you grabbed your knees and tried your hardest to prevent them from twisting.

Practice jumping was common on Sunday afternoons during the winter months. Large crowds of people accumulated at "Turtle" Lake for tobogganing, ice skating and to observe the jumpers. This was a huge "todo" for the local folk as the times of the depression were hard and this was a relatively inexpensive form of entertainment.

Once a year, the Hartford Ski Club hosted its own ski jumping tournament, drawing skiers from other clubs and around the world. Sverre Freidham, an Olympic skier in the 1930's, often showed to jump. Before the tournament began, Harold Skalstad and the other members of the Hartford Ski Club sang the classic, Norski ski jumping song, "Yumpin' Yiminee."

Concession stands sold hot dogs, coffee, hot chocolate and cigars. Local Hartford businessmen sponsored the jumpers.

The tournament's success primarily depended upon the winter snow. If snow was light, men hauled snow to the ramp by bushels. The winner of Classes A, B and C were honored later that evening at the Schwartz Park Pavilion where prizes were money, new skis or bragging rights. Dance orchestras, such as Pep Babler's Dance Orchestra, provided music, and young ladies hoped for the opportunity to dance with the risk-taking boys.

One year, after not winning a prize at the annual tournament, Elmo Halverson skied home from the jump. On the road, Rudy Pabst (of Pabst beer) pulled to a stop. Mr. Pabst asked Elmo if he had won any prizes. Elmo said, "No." At that time, Mr. Pabst gave Elmo a ten dollar bill. Elmo had won a prize after all.

When Erv Skalstad was 16, his father, Harold, was severely injured in a farming accident. While Harold did eventually recover, Erv dropped out of high school in order to oversee the running of the family farm. With new responsibilities upon him, Erv did not jump again, and the Hartford Ski Club was lost amidst the rising threat and needs of the war.

Sometime in the mid 1940's, while America was at war with Germany, wire was in great demand. The wires holding the ski jump were confiscated for better use. With the first strong wind, the ski jump toppled to the ground. Thus ended the era of the Hartford Ski Club.

Dr. Frederick Banting, a Canadian, originally noted his idea of isolating pancreatic ducts of dogs on October 31, 1920. Acquiring the research power of J.J.R. Macleod, thus began the frantic and maddening race to isolate and purify pancreatic secretions. On October 25, 1923, the Nobel Prize was awarded to these two men for their work. Dr. Banting and Mr. Macleod were not amicable however, and Banting declared he would share his prize with Mr. Charles

Best. In return, Macleod announced his sharing of the prize with Dr. J.B. Collip. Much controversy exists regarding these issues. Regardless of who did what, the clinical importance of insulin cannot be understated. The power of this medication to save lives exists still today.

"The Discovery of Insulin," by Michael Bliss. Copyright 1982 by Michael Bliss. The University of Chicago Press.

Kissel Kars were manufactured in Hartford by the Kissel Motor Car Company between the years of 1906-1931, a victim of the stark times of the depression. Gold Bug Speedsters were the most famous of the Kissel Kars, sporting the classic Kissel Kar yellow, nickel trim and bragging of fat-man wheels. The Gold Bug was adored by celebrities and owned by the likes of Amelia Earhart, Jack Dempsey, Al Jolson and Ralph De Palma. The last Gold Bug was manufactured in 1927. The Kissel Motor Car Company continued to make parts, outboard motors and some trucks for the war, but in 1942, the company was sold. Kissels and other early vehicles can be viewed within the Hartford Heritage Automobile Museum.
http://www.classicar.com/museums/hartford/hartford.html

On January 30, 1938, and for the fourth year in a row, the United States of America hosted its biggest social event of the year, the celebration of President Franklin Delano Roosevelt's birthday. Honoring President Roosevelt, over 5,000 communities held balls in which to raise monies to battle infantile and childhood paralysis. Hartford's ball was held within the Schwartz Ballroom. This octagonal ballroom has been a Hartford landmark for over fifty years

and has seen many popular big bands such as: Lawrence Welk, Woody Herman, the Dorsey Brothers and Guy Lombardo. The Schwartz, which is currently the Chandelier Ballroom, also served as a POW camp and venue for Vaudeville acts. It is now a common structure for wedding receptions and business functions, parties and other social events.
http://www.chandelierballroom.com

Heppe's Department Store sold foodstuffs and clothing for the local shoppers. Oftentimes during the depression, farmers bartered eggs in return for these items. Knoll's did sell a beautiful ladies wristwatch at $9.99 and A.A. Schmidt and Son offered a Voss LS, 2-Tub and Rinse, Electro-Safe washing machine for the low price of $39.95. Maas's meat market and Badger Pharmacy also aligned Main Street. The Hartford Times Press is in print to this day.

Perhaps one of Hartford's most famous historic landmarks, Holy Hill, the National Shrine of Mary, Help of Christians, stands atop a steep moulin kame, on the highest point of southeastern Wisconsin. The Discalced Carmelite Friars of Holy Hill oversee over 400 acres of protected natural woodlands. Visible amidst the rolling hills of the Kettle Moraine, and decorated by outstanding sculptures, stained glass windows and wildlife, Holy Hill is a breathtaking sight for both local folk and pilgrims.
http://www.holyhill.com

I wish to thank the following people in helping me to understand what it was like to live in the Hartford community during the 1930's: Erwin Skalstad, Elmo Halverson, Charlotte Feutz, Anita Roemer and Bob Campbell.

While talking to Erv one day in his kitchen, he said something that in my mind, clinched the story of this book.

I said, "My main character is a 15 year-old girl."

"Well Rachel," he said, "you do have to understand one thing. Girls don't jump."

And guess what? His use of the present-tense (at that time) was right, at least in terms of our Olympic Winter Games. Up through our 2010 Winter Games in Vancouver, British Columbia, Canada, women were not allowed to participate in ski jumping.

With incredible excitement and satisfaction, on April 6, 2011, the International Olympic Committee announced Women's Ski Jumping would be on the 2014 Olympic program in Sochi, Russia for the first time. According to Deedee Corradini, the Women's Ski Jumping USA president, 2014 will be the "first gender-equal Winter Games in Olympic history."

After hearing Erv's comment, "Girls don't jump," I shivered in my shoes. I knew Vivian would. Maybe nobody ever saw girls jump back then, but my guess is they did.

Perhaps shrouded in boys' clothing.
Perhaps by the light of the moon.

For more information about Rachel Callaray,
please visit www.callaray.com.

Made in the USA
Charleston, SC
12 April 2012